A Heart Unchained

BRIE'S SUBMISSION

Red Phoenix

A Heart Unchained:
Brie's Submission Book 23

Cover by Shanoff Designs
Formatted by BB eBooks
Phoenix symbol by Nicole Delfs

Dedication

I dedicate A Heart Unchained to the incredible muses in my head. I knew while writing Secrets of the Heart that they had a much bigger story to tell.

Writing this book has been pure joy! Each day I sat down to write another chapter and could barely keep up with my typing as the story played out in my mind.

There are so many touching moments in this book. You can bet I was crying with joy.

And the BDSM scenes?

Oh my, did I have fun writing those! I personally think there are two in here that may be my best yet. I know they got my motor revved.

Then there are the revelations we discover about several of our characters. I sobbed through those because their struggles hit me in the gut.

These people so much more than characters—they are like real people to me. Their pain is my pain. Their joy is my joy.

What I particularly love about this book is that there are little nuggets of goodness that have been sprinkled throughout this book, which you won't appreciate until later on. My jaw dropped quite a few times while writing it, and I seriously can't wait for you to experience those moments when you reread this book in the future.

The deeper we get into Brie's story, the more I cherish the genius of the muses.

I have to give a huge shout out to Kh Koehler. This book took a while to formulate in my head, so by the time I was ready to write, it came out like a hurricane. I kept throwing my chapters at her while I jumped to the next. It was a tough schedule, but she was right by my side and her edits…just wow! She knows my voice and was able to make this book sing. I'm indebted to her.

I also want to give huge thanks to MrRed. When the time came to sink everything I had into A Heart Unchained, he took care of me—making sure I was fed, decorating the house for Trismas, and adding some inspiration to the hot scenes (if you know what I mean).

Then there are my proofers, Becki, Brenda, and Marilyn. They faithfully work beside me each book to help catch those pesky errors that escape. I have to say, I ate up their reactions to this book. It was like opening little presents each time I got an email while they were reading.

My dear fans, I must also dedicate this book to you.

I had no idea when I wrote about Brie's first day at the Submissive Training Center that I would connect with a bunch of incredible people. Brie has brought us together over the years (Dec 13th, 2021 marked my 10 year publiversary) and I will be forever grateful for you.

Here's to Brie and the gang! May they continue to thrill us for years to come.

SIGN UP FOR MY NEWSLETTER HERE FOR THE LATEST RED PHOENIX UPDATES

FOLLOW ME ON INSTAGRAM
INSTAGRAM.COM/REDPHOENIXAUTHOR

SALES, GIVEAWAYS, NEW RELEASES, PREORDER LINKS, AND MORE!

SIGN UP HERE
REDPHOENIXAUTHOR.COM/NEWSLETTER-SIGNUP

CONTENTS

Morning Surprises

B rie woke up to the sound of a crow cawing just outside the bedroom window.

As she listened to the crow's impassioned cries, she wondered if it was rejoicing with her over her victory against Greg Holloway the night before, or if its call was meant as a warning. Although crows were considered bad omens by some, Brie knew the birds were highly intelligent creatures, and she had great respect for them.

Glancing at Sir, Brie couldn't help but smile. He looked so handsome sleeping beside her, a peaceful expression on his face. While she lay there admiring him, he opened his eyes.

"Good morning, babygirl."

The sound of his voice was like a warm blanket to her soul. She grinned, leaning in to kiss him. "It is a *very* good morning, Sir."

"Still flying high after last night's triumph?"

Brie sighed in contentment. "I still can't believe it's real…" She lay back against the pillow and grinned up at the ceiling. "My documentary is going to be produced by the best talent in Hollywood. After being shunned for so long, I can't quite wrap my head around it!"

"People should never underestimate you…" he growled as he claimed her lips. He then left a slow trail of kisses down her throat as he began caressing her breasts.

"Oh, Sir," Brie purred, closing her eyes as she gave in to the sensual shivers his touch inspired. After last night's reenactment of their first scene together, Brie's body was quick to respond to his attention.

"Up for a morning session before the children wake, téa?" he asked, raising an eyebrow seductively before he encased her nipple with his lips.

She felt the welcome ache in her loins as he began sucking on it and moaned, "If it pleases you, Master…"

His hand immediately slipped under the covers. Brie gushed with wetness as his talented fingers began teasing her clit.

To her surprise, he pulled away and got up. Walking to her side of the bed, he ripped off the covers and picked her up, carrying her over to the tantra chair in the corner. Laying her on it, he ordered her to spread her legs while he quickly rid himself of his boxers.

Kneeling beside her, he resumed his attention on her nipples as he lovingly caressed her pussy.

"Morning sex is the best," she murmured.

"The perfect way to start a new day," he agreed, his voice gruff as he pressed his finger into her wet pussy.

Brie arched her back, loving his intimate penetration as he started stroking her G-spot with his finger.

"Already wet and ready for me," he growled huskily.

She let out a purr of satisfaction. "Yes…"

Increasing the rhythm and pressure of his finger, Sir kissed her breasts before refocusing his attention on her lips.

Having her nipples sucked while he stimulated her G-spot was incredibly arousing. Moaning into his mouth, she felt the fluttering of an impending orgasm. "I'm close," she confessed.

"I know…" he murmured huskily. "I want you to come."

With permission given, Brie threw her head back and let the building tension take over as Sir explored her mouth with his tongue. He knew her body well and quickly took Brie to the edge, but knowing he wanted the orgasm to be intense, she held off from giving in fully to her climax.

Instead, she closed her eyes and concentrated on the pleasure his fingers and lips were bringing. When she felt she could take no more, she cried out and embraced the climax. Brie's whole body shuddered as it consumed her, erasing all other thoughts.

"That's it, babygirl," Sir praised, kissing her deeply until the orgasm subsided. He left her for a moment and returned with the Magic Wand. Plugging it in, he handed her the tool before straddling the tantra chair. His hard cock stood at the perfect height for her to kiss.

Grasping his shaft, she placed a tender kiss on the head before taking it into her mouth. The sound of his low groan turned her on.

"Play with yourself as you suck me," he commanded.

Brie switched on the powerful vibrator and dutifully pressed it against her clit. The intensity of the vibration caused her to let out a muffled moan as she continued to suck her Master's cock.

She was rewarded with the taste of his precome, letting her know he was as turned on as she was. Brie eagerly sucked his rigid shaft while the vibrator had its way with her clit. She experienced a unique synergy caused by the intense stimulation of the wand while sucking his cock. It seemed the one enhanced the other, making the slow build of her next orgasm deliciously pleasurable.

Sir pressed his shaft deeper down her throat, matching the rhythm of the sensual pulses the wand was creating. The dual sensation was something Brie couldn't get enough of. It didn't take long before her hips lifted of their own accord, and she was rocked by an orgasm that stole her breath away.

She quickly turned off the vibrator and closed her eyes for a moment, riding the orgasm to completion while she continued sucking his cock. When Sir pulled away, she smiled, looking up at him demurely.

His eyes flashed with ravenous desire. "I want to fuck that pussy."

"Please, Master," she begged.

"From behind," he ordered, holding out his hand to her. Brie took his hand and stood up, trembling with anticipation as she settled on the higher end of the tantra chair, waiting for him to claim her.

Wrapping one hand around her waist, Sir guided his cock with the other, pressing it into her opening. Having just orgasmed powerfully, her pussy was tight but incredibly wet.

"Yes!" she cried when he thrust his shaft deep into her.

Normally, Sir delayed his own climax, but this morning he gave in to his need, taking her hard and fast. She loved his deep thrusts and had to cover her mouth to muffle her cries, not wanting to wake the children, when she came once again.

Pulling out, Sir slapped her soundly on the ass, enjoying the gush of her watery come. Slipping his cock back inside her, he growled possessively as he ramped up his thrusts again.

Brie whimpered in pure pleasure, loving the force of his strokes. When he stopped for a moment, her inner muscles squeezed his cock tightly and she came a third time.

"Hungry for your Master, are you?" he chuckled.

She turned her head and grinned at him lustfully. "Always."

"Then let me fill you," he said in a low, sensual voice.

This time, Sir thrust even deeper as he prepared to come. Brie heard his masculine groan as he climaxed inside her, and she stilled her body so she could feel it.

Brie was surprised when she experienced a delayed orgasm afterwards, when he wrapped his arms around her with his cock still deep inside.

Sir nuzzled her neck. "I love feeling you come."

That's when she heard the hungry cries of the baby coming from the nursery. Brie instantly felt an ache in her breasts in response to the sound. "Couldn't have timed that any better," she panted.

"I aim to please," he replied huskily, smacking her on the ass one last time before standing up to throw on his sweatpants. "I'll get Anthony while you freshen up."

She smiled, touched by his thoughtfulness. "Thank you, Sir."

He winked at her. "The perfect way to start our day."

Still flying on the high of their sexual tryst, Brie glanced at her reflection in the mirror and smiled to herself. Last night had been a huge victory for her career. One she and Mary had fought hard for…

Her heart skipped a beat the moment she thought about Mary. The girl was her rival when she first enrolled in The Submissive Training Center, but now Mary was one of her most loyal friends.

Sadly, because of the way last night played out, Mary felt betrayed, believing Brie had broken her vow to keep silent about Greg Holloway's abuse.

Although Brie had seriously considered breaking that promise many times, out of love for Mary and respect for their friendship, she had opted to keep an uneasy silence.

But, last night, after Sir and Marquis witnessed Holloway's true nature for themselves, they'd rescued Mary from his clutches. Instead of being grateful for her freedom, Mary had turned on Brie.

On some primal level, Brie understood the reason why. As a child, Mary had been betrayed by her mother and the man she thought was her father.

After her mother abandoned her to save herself,

Mary endured unimaginable physical abuse at the hands of the man who raised her. It made sense that Mary saw the whole world as a threat.

To protect herself, Mary was abrasive and cruel to anyone who dared get too close. That Mary had let Brie into her inner circle was a miracle by itself, and it broke Brie's heart that Mary felt she had been betrayed once again.

Heading to the kitchen, Brie started a pot of green tea because she needed to soothe her soul. Although her tea never quite matched that of Tono's, sipping it always brought the kinbaku master to her mind.

Brie closed her eyes, seeing his warm smile and the glint in his chocolate brown eyes. Nodding, she whispered to herself as she took a sip of her tea, "I will go to Mary, Tono. However, I need your calming spirit with me today when I speak to her."

Mary needed to know the truth before it crumbled the tenuous foundation of their friendship.

Sir walked into the room carrying Anthony in one arm and a sleepy Hope in the other. "They both wanted to see their mama."

Hope rubbed her eyes, then held out her arms to Brie.

Leaning in to rub noses with her, Brie asked, "Did your little brother wake you up, sweet pea?"

Kissing Hope on the head, Brie took Anthony from Sir so she could feed her crying son. She let out a nervous sigh as she sat down on the couch.

"What wrong, babygirl?" Sir asked, chuckling lightly. "You were smiling just a moment ago."

Brie looked at him sadly. "I'm worried about Mary."

He walked to the couch and sat beside her, setting Hope on his lap. "There is no reason to worry about Miss Wilson's safety. She is in capable hands."

"It's not that…" Her heart beat faster knowing the time had come to tell Sir the truth. Brie always knew there would be a price to be paid for her silence…

Mary Quite Contrary

B rie was nervous, forcing herself to meet Sir's gaze. "I have to see Mary."

Sir shook his head in response. "We leave for Russia soon. Surely, it can wait."

"No, it can't. Mary thinks I betrayed her."

He furrowed his brow in confusion. "Why would she think that?"

Before answering, Brie lay Anthony down and went to the pantry. She returned with a bag of rice in her hand. Kneeling on the floor before him, she bowed her head.

"What is the meaning of this, Brie?" he asked, his tone suddenly cold.

Keeping her head lowered, she answered, "I have kept something from you. I made a promise to Mary and could not break her confidence."

"Go on," he demanded.

Brie looked up at him hesitantly, her stomach twisting into knots. "I promised her I wouldn't tell anyone—

not even you—about the abuse she was suffering at Holloway's hands."

Sir's gaze penetrated her soul. "Why on Earth would you promise such a thing when you knew it could put her life in danger?"

"Mary threatened to hurt herself if I didn't." Her bottom lip trembled when she added, "I begged her to speak to you, but she refused to listen to me."

Sir stared at her without saying a word.

The silence was unbearable.

"I had no choice, Sir. Either way, I believed Mary's life was in danger."

Brie expected to see anger reflected in his eyes but, to her surprise, she saw a look of compassion. Nodding thoughtfully, he told her, "Miss Wilson put you in a difficult position." He sighed, sounding troubled. "She might have followed through on that threat if you had broken that confidence."

Taking the bag of rice from her, Sir set it on the counter. "There is an aspect of Miss Wilson's past that you were not made aware of during training. We did not require her to share it with others."

"What is that, Sir?"

"She admitted during her training that she attempted suicide as a teenager."

"Poor Mary," Brie exclaimed sadly. She could only imagine the pain Mary must have suffered as a teenager.

Sir looked at her with concern. "If Miss Wilson truly believes you betrayed her last night, she may follow through with that threat. I will call Captain and apprise him of the situation while you ask your parents if they can care for the children. It's important that Miss Wilson hear the truth from you as soon as possible."

A flood of relief rushed through her. "I agree, Sir."

Not long after getting dressed, Brie was surprised to hear the doorbell ring. She opened the door to find both her parents standing there. Her mother's face looked as white as a sheet.

"How the heck did you get here so fast?"

"Your father drove like a maniac…" her mother whimpered.

"I only kept up with the other idiots on the road, Marcy," he corrected. "Not my fault California drivers treat the roads like their personal raceway."

Looking at Brie, he added, "I could hear the fear in your voice, little girl, when you told me it was important and I got here as fast as I could."

Brie threw her arms around her dad, deeply touched. "Thank you, Daddy!"

He patted her gently as he hugged her, whispering, "I'd do anything to help you, Brianna."

She was overwhelmed by the love and concern she felt in his embrace, but he quickly pulled away and ordered, "Now, go! You have somewhere to be, and we have grandkids to spoil."

Brie laughed softly, giving her mother a quick hug before following Sir out the door.

On the drive to Captain's house, she asked Sir, "How did Captain say Mary was doing?"

Sir pursed his lips. "Mary refuses to speak to him and has locked herself in the guestroom."

Brie felt chills hearing that. Captain and Candy had

offered their home to Mary after seeing what transpired with Holloway last night. Of all the people she knew, Brie thought Captain was the one person Mary would confide in.

"Is he sure she's okay?"

"Yes. Although she may not want to speak to him, she is being quite vocal in her hatred of him."

Brie groaned, imagining the undeserved insults being leveled at Captain. However, she was deeply relieved to hear Mary was safe.

"That hatred will soon be focused on you," Sir warned her. "You cannot take anything she says to heart."

Now, she felt nervous about seeing Mary.

However, she was grateful for his reminder. Brie knew she was the only person Mary trusted—Mary had even risked her life for her. But now that Mary felt betrayed by her, Brie fully expected she would pay the price for every person who'd ever hurt Mary.

Those concerns were confirmed the moment she got out of the car and heard Mary screaming from inside the house. She blushed at the filthy words Mary was spewing at Captain and Candy. Mary was so loud, one of the neighbors watering his lawn asked them, "Do you think I should call the police?"

Sir shook his head, chuckling lightly. "That won't be necessary, I assure you."

Turning to Brie, he said in a low voice, "If you need me at any point during your conversation with Mary, you have only to call out. I will be standing on the other side of the door."

Brie sighed nervously. "I'm sure it'll be fine, but I appreciate that, Sir."

When Sir rang the doorbell, Candy answered it with a sweet smile despite the profanity echoing from the hallway behind her.

"Please come in!"

Brie looked at Candy with sympathy. "I'm sorry Mary is taking this out on you when you've been nothing but kind to her."

After Candy closed the door, she shrugged and told Brie, "I realize Mary's anger is misplaced." Glancing down the hallway, "I hope it helps Mary release the pain she has kept buried."

Brie stared at Candy in awe, touched by her words. Instead of being offended by Mary's unkind verbal assault, Candy had chosen to ignore the abuse because she understood Mary's anger was not actually directed at her.

"I hope that once I have a chance to talk with Mary, things will calm down," Brie told her.

Candy reached out and squeezed Brie's hand. "She is lucky to have you as a friend, Brianna."

Captain was standing outside the guestroom door and nodded to Brie when she approached. From behind the door, Mary screeched, "And another thing, you fucking geezer, you think you're all high and mighty…but you're far from being a saint. Hell, you're worse than Greg!" She beat her fists against the door in anger. "At least *he* embraces who he is!"

When Captain failed to respond, Mary ramped it up a notch. "Yeah, you go around pretending to be a war hero like you deserve respect, but we all know the truth. While your men were fighting for their fucking lives, you deserted them to save your own skin. There's no other explanation for the captain in charge of so many men to be the only one to survive a battle."

Captain winced. Placing a hand over his eyepatch, he closed his other eye as grief washed over him. Brie was certain he was reliving the day his men were killed, and she resented Mary for causing him that kind of pain.

When he opened his eye, Captain met Brie's gaze with a look of compassion. "If all you've ever known growing up is pain and betrayal, it's hard to imagine there is any other reality, and it colors everything she sees."

Brie nodded in understanding.

Captain knocked on the door and waited until Mary took a breath between her cursing. "Mrs. Davis is here, lief. She would like to talk to you."

"That fucking whore?" Mary screeched like a banshee. "I don't want anything to do with that cunt!"

"Let me rephrase that," Captain replied calmly. "Unlock the door. Mrs. Davis has come to speak with you."

"No! That lying piece of shit isn't getting anywhere near me." Mary pounded the door with her fists. "You hear me, motherfucker?"

"Lief, I will not ask again. Unlock the door now," Captain commanded.

Brie was thankful Captain still had power over Mary.

A few moments later, she heard the door unlock.

"Come in, Brie…" Mary stated in an icy voice that chilled Brie to the bone.

Frightened by the ominous tone in her voice, Brie

hesitated for a moment. When she finally went to turn the doorknob, Sir reached out and grabbed her wrist to stop her. "You don't have to go in alone."

She looked into his eyes when she explained, "Yes, I do. Under all that rage and fury is a little girl who is hurt. This is the only way she'll listen to me."

He nodded, reminding her, "I'll be right outside." Glancing at Captain, he added, "We both will."

Brie faced the door and breathed in deep, letting it out slowly as she thought of Tono. "Just breathe…" she murmured to herself.

The instant she stepped through the door, she was hit with the power of Mary's rage. It was like another person in the room. The intensity of her fury was both palpable and real.

"You have a lot of nerve coming here," Mary growled in that same low, ominous tone. It didn't even sound like her. "I can't decide if you are an idiot or a fool."

When Brie met her lethal gaze she froze for a moment, struggling to remain calm. "Aren't they the same thing?"

"No," Mary snarled. "A fool walks into a situation due to ignorance. An idiot does it out of arrogance." She raised an eyebrow, a cruel sneer on her lips. "Which is it, bitch?"

"I came out of love."

Her word surprised Mary, but instead of quenching the fires, it only seemed to fan them. Mary walked up to her, her malice growing heavier with each step.

Brie suddenly felt like an insect caught in a spider's

web.

"Love doesn't exist in this world," Mary stated, glaring at Brie. "Fool me once, shame on you. Fool me twice, shame on me." Her expression grew even uglier. "And I'm no fool."

Goosebumps rose on Brie's skin.

Breathe…

Brie was deathly afraid that one false move on her part would end this encounter and she might never see Mary again. "I didn't break my vow to you."

Brie's words acted like gas on a fire. Mary's eyes flashed with indignation before they darkened to a frightening hue. Without warning, Mary slapped her cheek and screamed, "How dare you lie to my face!"

Brie rubbed her stinging cheek, stating earnestly, "I never lied to you."

"The fuck you didn't!"

"Mary, Marquis Gray, and Sir saw how Holloway was treating you last night. Hell, the entire room saw it."

Mary balled her hands into fists, looking as if she was getting ready to pummel Brie.

Rather than defend herself, Brie took another deep breath and thought of the kinbaku Master while she braced for an attack. Suddenly, a sense of peace washed over her as if Tono were standing beside her.

Looking directly into her eyes, Brie smiled at Mary. "You did it. You said you would fucking do it, and you did."

Mary's eyes narrowed. "What the hell are you talking about?"

"You beat Greg Holloway. You told me you would,

and last night you took the fucker down."

Instead of being pacified, Mary howled in rage. "You don't get it, you moron! You have no idea what you have unleashed, and I have no way to stop him now."

Brie threw her arms around Mary, suddenly understanding that her friend's anger was coming from a place of fear for her safety. "This isn't your fight anymore, Mary. You did what you needed to do."

To her surprise, Mary's face suddenly contorted with sorrow. Clutching Brie, Mary buried her face against Brie's shoulder and started crying.

Mumbling into Brie's shirt, she cried, "He's going to bury you…"

"No," Brie stated with conviction, hugging Mary even tighter. "You forget—we are not alone. We have the entire Submissive Training Center behind us."

Mary groaned, pulling away from Brie. "It's not going to be enough, Stinks. You have no clue what Greg is capable of."

Brie caught the haunted look in Mary's eyes and immediately hugged her again, stating emphatically, "Last night, Greg's balls were effectively cut off in the eyes of all of Hollywood. He has no power over us anymore."

Mary shook her head sadly at Brie as if she didn't believe it.

Disturbance

By calling in a favor from one of his long-time clients, Sir managed to book a first-class suite for the long flight to Russia so they could sleep comfortably with the children.

Brie was a bundle of excitement because Sir had insisted on surprising Rytsar, so the sexy sadist had no idea they were coming!

Although Rytsar had been there for Anthony's birth via video chat, he'd had to watch it from Moscow. Knowing how much he loved being a *dyadya*, Brie couldn't wait for the moment Rytsar held him for the first time. She was also extremely curious what Russian nickname he would give their son.

"I'm so excited!" she told Sir as they packed for the extended trip.

Sir admitted, "It will ease my mind greatly to check on Durov and Wallace in person." There was a glint in his eye when he added, "But, to see the look on Nonna's face when she holds her great-grandson—that is the icing on the cake for me."

Brie gushed, "I bet your entire family will be there when we arrive."

Sir nodded, but a sad look came to his eyes. "My grandparents were hit hard when their only son died. It does my heart good to give them this little bit of happiness."

She realized how important it was to Sir and said as she hugged him, "It will be good for all of us."

As he leaned down to give her a kiss, his cell phone rang. "Don't move," he ordered. When Sir saw who was calling, a smile spread across his face. Putting it on speaker so she could hear, he said, "Don't tell me your precious cat is pregnant again, Anderson? I hate to tell you, but I haven't seen Shadow in days."

Brie put her hands to her mouth to keep from laughing as she stared at Shadow sitting only a few feet away, watching them pack.

"*What?* You let that unneutered bastard roam free?"

"There's no reason to be alarmed," Sir stated as Shadow got up and brushed up against his leg. "But you might want to check to make sure there aren't any holes in your outdoor catio…just in case."

"Ah, hell. Don't even go there."

"If he made his way inside, I'm certain it was a romantic coupling."

Master Anderson growled. "You like messing with me, don't you, buddy?"

"I do," Sir admitted, winking at Brie.

Brie smiled as Shadow sauntered over to the suitcase to check it out.

"What was the reason for the call?" Sir asked.

"I was wondering if you could swing by for a bit. There's something…important I'd like to talk to you about."

"Unfortunately, we're headed to Russia tonight and then on to Italy to visit my family."

Master Anderson chuckled warmly. "I like hearing that from you. Family is important."

"Agreed." Sir smiled at Brie. "If it's pressing, you are certainly welcome to come to the house while we pack."

"Nah, it can wait until you return. You give your grandparents a hug for me."

After hanging up, Sir walked into the closet, returning with the stylish box that held the mask Dante had made for her. "We can't forget this for the trip."

She trembled when she saw it, wondering what he had planned for that mask. Sir knew exactly how to make Brie crazy with anticipation.

Lifting her chin, he murmured, "Now, where was I…"

Brie stared at the huge jet they would be boarding soon and laughed. "It's hard to believe something that huge can even get off the ground."

Sir's voice was stiff when he replied, "Human ingenuity is remarkable."

Looking at him with sympathy, she asked, "It's hard every time we fly, isn't it?"

"I won't deny it. However, it damn well beats taking days to get there by boat and train," Sir chuckled lightly.

Hefting Hope onto his shoulders, he forced a smile as he walked toward the gate. Brie followed behind him, excited to be traveling again despite Sir's misgivings about flying. Knowing they would be seeing Rytsar soon had her flying on cloud nine.

Thankfully, the takeoff out of LAX was uneventful. Once they were safely in the air, Brie could see Sir beginning to visibly relax.

Traveling at night made it easy with two young children. Brie glanced over at Sir and her heart skipped a beat. There was nothing cuter than seeing him hold Hope, her head resting against his shoulder as she slept soundly.

"You are a wonderful father, Mr. Davis," she told him.

Unlike the trips in her past, there would be no kinky scenes with Sir on this flight. Glancing down at her son sleeping peacefully in her arms, Brie found she didn't mind one bit. She loved being a mom and Anthony was perfect—just like his daddy.

Whenever Anthony began to fuss, Brie walked up and down the aisle of the large plane. He seemed lulled by the movement and the constant drone of the engines. It wasn't until they were a few hours out of Moscow that he suddenly became inconsolable.

Heading back to her seat, Brie sat down to feed Anthony. While he was nursing, the stewardess knocked on the cabin door. When Sir opened it, she asked what they would like to drink.

With no warning, the plane suddenly lurched and the woman fell forward. Sir grasped her with one hand to steady her while still holding tight to Hope with the other. Looking out the window, Brie was surprised to see not a single cloud in the sky.

The stewardess laughed nervously as she apologized to Sir. Then it lurched again, and the airplane was tossed violently. Brie clutched Anthony as she watched in horror as the drink cart hit the ceiling and drinks went everywhere. The poor stewardess flew up, hitting the ceiling hard at the same time the oxygen masks fell from above.

Brie's stomach twisted when the airplane dipped and began falling at an alarming rate. Someone on the plane screamed, "I don't want to die!"

Sir turned to Brie, sandwiching the two children between them as he wrapped his powerful arms around her. "I've got you."

A sense of calm washed over her when she looked into his eyes. Even if these were her last moments, she was where she wanted to be—in Sir's arms. Although she mourned the future her children would never have, Brie felt no fear.

As suddenly as the turbulence hit, it stopped and the plane righted itself, slowly rising back into the sky. Brie let out a frightened gasp, shocked that they were still alive. "Sir…"

"Are you okay?" he asked her.

Stunned, she could only nod.

Giving her a quick kiss, Sir unbuckled his seatbelt and got up from his seat to help the stewardess who lay crumpled on the floor.

The pilot spoke over the intercom, his voice high-pitched and shaky. "Folks, we just passed through a band of clear air turbulence. Although unpredictable, they are known to happen this time of year. Now that we've passed through the band, I don't anticipate any further disturbances. However, I ask that you remain in your seats with your seatbelts on for the duration of this flight."

Brie kissed the tops of her crying children's heads, her entire body trembling from the rush of endorphins. What she was experiencing was similar to a sub-high, but in this case, it was caused by the certainty that death had been averted.

When Sir sat back down beside her, she looked at him, both grateful and frightened. He smiled at her reassuringly and reached out to play with her hair just as he would during aftercare.

Neither of them said a word during the rest of the flight, but when they finally landed, Brie joined the others on the plane as they broke out in relieved applause. As they deplaned, the captain stood with his cockpit crew to see the passengers off. He shook the hand of each person as they passed.

"Thank you," Sir said in a gruff voice as he clasped the pilot's hand and shook it firmly.

Brie noticed tears in the captain's eyes when he glanced at their two children while shaking her hand.

"Thank you for saving my family," she told him fervently.

He nodded to her, too choked up to speak.

Brie walked off the plane in a daze. Once she reached the terminal, she scanned all the people at the airport running about. While they were focused on making their flights, she was simply grateful to be alive.

Sir informed her that he needed to use the bathroom. While she waited outside the lavatory, she heard the distinct sound of him retching and her heart broke. Although he had remained calm throughout the entire flight, she knew he'd just lived his greatest nightmare.

When he walked back out, he nodded to her and lifted Hope into his arms, the picture of calm. "Let's get our bags and get the hell out of this place."

Syurpriz!

S ir hailed a taxi and they started a slow and tedious trip as they crawled through morning traffic to reach the modern and stylish high-rises of Moskva-City.

Brie sighed in frustration and turned to Sir. "Rytsar starts his mornings early. Do you think he'll still be there when we arrive?"

He smiled when he answered, "While Durov may have no idea we're coming, Maxim does. He'll make certain Durov stays put until we get there."

After what had just happened, Brie was even more impatient to reunite with him. As she looked at their two children, a shiver when down her spine. If it hadn't been for the skill of the pilot, none of them would be here right now. In one fell swoop, the Alonzo Davis family line would have been completely erased.

"Try not to think of it, babygirl," Sir advised, wrapping his arm around her.

Brie laid her head on his shoulder. She had only experienced a momentary scare, while Sir had been forced to relive the horror he'd experienced the day his plane crashed in LA. "Are you all right, Sir?"

He squeezed her tighter. "I will be."

She pulled away, looking at him with concern. "Maybe we shouldn't have come."

"It's important we're here. Now lay your head back down and do your best to forget it. Durov and Wallace don't need to know what happened on the flight."

She agreed, knowing how Rytsar and Faelan would react if she told them. It would serve no purpose to burden them with the knowledge.

"It'll be our little secret," Brie promised, grateful their children were too young to remember it.

Pointing to the tall, artistic buildings of Moskva-City, Brie told Hope, "Your *dyadya* lives here."

Hope perked up. "Dyadya?"

"Yes, little angel. Your *dyadya* is up in that building right there," Sir told her.

Hope started bouncing in her seat and clapping her hands together. Brie smiled, touched by her daughter's infectious joy and innocence. What happened on the plane was now in the past for her little girl and had no bearing on her excitement about seeing Rytsar.

Following Sir's advice and Hope's example, Brie set her sights on the building as they approached, pushing out all other thoughts.

By the time they reached the top floor in the elevator, Brie's heart started racing with anticipation. Sir knocked on the door and stood back to wait. When Maxim answered, she could hear a television blasting in the background.

As soon as Maxim saw the four of them, he pursed his lips in amusement and closed the door, stating loudly in Russian, "*Gospodin,* there is a delivery from the US."

Brie heard Rytsar rant from behind the door. "Why are you telling me? Sign for it and bring it to me."

"I cannot."

"*Blyat!*"

Brie grinned when she heard Rytsar continue to curse as he approached the door. "First, you delay me this morning with nonsense, and now this? I should fire you and get a new man."

Cradling Anthony in her arms, Brie bit her lip as she waited for Rytsar to open the door. The moment he did, Hope reached out to him, crying, "Dyadya!"

The grin on Rytsar's face was priceless as he automatically reached for the child. "I can't believe this…" he sputtered in complete shock, shaking his head at Sir.

It took him a short moment to realize Brie was there as well.

"*Radost moya…*" he murmured, then looked at the infant in her arms. Brie's smile grew as she unwrapped the baby from the blanket so he could see him.

Rytsar's grin grew as she held her son. "*Moy gordost.*"

Brie's bottom lip quivered when she heard the special name he had for their baby.

My pride…

"Come in!" he insisted. "I must be properly introduced to my godson."

Kissing Hope on the cheek, he handed her back to Sir before taking the tiny infant from Brie's arms. Rocking him gently, the burly Russian smiled down at their son, stating in Russian, "You are handsome, brave, and strong."

It felt almost as if Rytsar were granting those attributes to their son. He smiled at her, explaining, "I was told those were the first words my mother said to me when I was born."

Brie nodded with tears in her eyes.

Glancing at Sir, Rytsar said, "I'm heartily grateful for this unexpected visit, *moy droog.*"

"We needed it as much as you, brother."

"You make beautiful children together." Rytsar grinned, draping an arm around Sir. "And, now, you only have three more to go."

Sir shook his head, chuckling.

"How was the flight?" Rytsar asked, releasing Sir to rub the top of Hope's curly head. "It must have been a challenge with two children in tow."

Sir didn't miss a beat when he answered. "The quarters were spacious. No complaints."

"That is good to hear."

"Dyadya," Hope called to him, wanting all of Rytsar's attention.

Rytsar obliged, handing Anthony back to Brie. He picked up Hope and twirled her in the air, inciting a string of delighted giggles.

"…the pilot averted near disaster when the American jet hit clear turbulence en route to Moscow…" emanated from the large TV.

Rytsar suddenly stopped and stared at the large screen while a video of the injured stewardess being wheeled on a gurney to a waiting ambulance popped on the screen.

The Russian turned to Sir, cocking his head. "Was that your flight, *moy droog?*"

When Sir failed to reply, Rytsar's eyes narrowed. "*Moy droog.*"

"It was."

Rytsar glanced at Brie, his expression changing as the reality of what almost happened washed over him. He shook his head, a bereft look on his face.

"It's not important," Sir stated emphatically. "We're fine."

"*Not important?*" Rytsar shouted.

"What's going on?" Faelan muttered as he staggered into the room with Little Sparrow by his side. She wagged her tail when she spotted the new visitors.

Brie was disheartened to see that Faelan still looked gaunt, his face drawn and haunted.

Rytsar immediately picked up the remote and turned off the TV. "The Davis's have come for a visit."

Faelan glanced at Sir and nodded before turning his attention on Brie. The moment his gaze landed on the baby, all color drained from his face.

"I can't…do this," he muttered, heading toward the front door with Little Sparrow dutifully following behind him.

"Faelan," Brie called out, but he didn't even look back as he shut the door. She gave Rytsar a worried look. "I thought he was doing better."

"The babe has thrown him. While he has moments of clarity, they are sporadic, *radost moya*. The boy needs more time."

"I'm certain that seeing our infant only reminded Wallace of his loss," Sir said with regret.

"It's good for him to confront reality," Rytsar assured him. "Speaking of reality…" His eyes narrowed again. "Why did you lie to me?"

Meeting his intense gaze, Sir stated, "I did not lie, old friend. I simply kept unnecessary details from you."

"I almost lost you all!" the Russian growled. "When exactly *did* you plan on telling me?"

Sir inclined his head and shrugged. "Never."

Rytsar snarled. "I'm not a babe that must be coddled."

"But you have enough to worry about," Brie explained.

Picking up on the sudden tension in the room, Hope looked up at Rytsar and began to cry.

Crushing her against his chest, Rytsar murmured gently, "No tears, *moya solntse*…" Kissing the top of her head, he choked out, "I could not have borne the loss."

"Which is why I chose to say nothing," Sir replied.

Rytsar stared at Sir and suddenly frowned. "You faced death again today, *moy droog*. Such an experience scars a man, even if he refuses to acknowledge it."

He then turned to Brie. "And you stared death in the face, *radost moya*."

She nodded, the reality of the near-fatal crash still too fresh for her to reconcile.

"I know what we need," Rytsar declared.

Brie fully expected him to say vodka. Instead, he ordered, "Maxim, clear my schedule for the morning."

"Already done, *gospodin*."

"Excellent." Rytsar handed Hope to him. "The three of us will be indisposed for the next hour."

Understanding suddenly flooded through Brie, and she quickly swaddled Anthony before setting him in the infant carrier. "If he begins to fuss, just rock him in it. He loves to be rocked."

Maxim nodded curtly.

Brie took the hand that Sir offered her and followed Rytsar as he walked down the hallway to his bedroom. This encounter wasn't about sex—this was about connection. Something the three of them desperately needed.

Russian Love

R ytsar opened the double doors to his bedroom and gestured for them to enter. Brie immediately noticed that he had changed the décor from the last time she'd been here. The modern furniture was covered in rich black leather, and he'd added stylish accent lighting that shone against the walls in shades of yellow, blue, and purple. But, the piece that dominated the bedroom was the incredibly large four-poster bed.

"Wow," she murmured in awe as she entered the room.

"I needed a change," Rytsar stated matter-of-factly.

Sir nodded his approval as he looked at the unusual bed.

"I had it specially made to comfortably fit three active people," he told them with a charming smirk.

Without warning, Rytsar picked Brie up and tossed her on the bed. She squealed in surprise, then laughed as she landed with a bounce on the springy bed.

Shutting the doors, the Russian turned to face her as

he began to slowly strip off his clothing. "I had no idea when I woke up this morning that I would be introducing you to my new bed, *radost moya*."

Glancing at Sir, he added, "*Moy droog*, pick a tool from the wall."

Sir walked to Rytsar's impressive set of BDSM tools. Grabbing a pair of leather cuffs, he tossed them to Rytsar, then took a riding crop from the wall. "Prepare her while I undress."

Brie felt tingles of excitement as Rytsar ripped off the last of his clothing and joined her on the bed with the cuffs dangling from his hand. She experienced the exhilarating sense of being caught as he grabbed her right leg and pulled her toward him.

She squeaked as he positioned his naked body on top of her and forcefully lifted one wrist above her head.

With quick movements, he buckled the cuff to her wrist and then smiled in satisfaction when he grabbed the other one. "There is no point in resisting," he growled teasingly.

Brie felt a gush of wetness between her legs when he finished securing her wrists and looked down at her. "How does it feel to be completely helpless with two men?"

She looked up into his lustful gaze and purred, "I love it."

Sir joined her on the other side of the bed, asking Rytsar, "Why didn't you undress her?"

The Russian's eyes glinted mischievously. "It is by design, comrade." With that, he grabbed her blouse with both hands and ripped it open. Brie gasped as buttons went flying everywhere.

His rough treatment was such a turn-on.

"I see a neck that needs my attention." Pressing her cuffed wrists into the bed, Rytsar changed position and leaned down, his teeth grazing her skin.

Sir was playfully rough as well as he undid her pants and forcefully pulled them down to her ankles. Brie pretended to struggle when he slipped his hand under her panties and rubbed her clit.

"Fuck…" he growled, his voice low and possessive as he pressed his finger into her. "She's wet."

"Of course, she is," Rytsar murmured ravenously, reaching under her bra to play with her breast. While he rolled her hard nipple between his fingers, Sir slipped two fingers inside her and began to tease her G-spot.

"You are our plaything," Rytsar informed her.

"Yes…Rytsar," she panted in enthusiastic agreement.

Brie lost herself in their aggressive foreplay, loving the undivided attention of both men.

At one point, Sir flipped her onto her stomach, making Brie yelp in excitement. He pulled down her panties just enough to slide his hard cock between her ass cheeks. He teased her with the head of his shaft but did not take her.

Instead, he pulled away and ripped off her jeans and panties, ordering her to get on her hands and knees. When she did not move quickly enough because of her bindings, he playfully snapped the crop across her ass.

Brie smiled when she felt the sting. Looking at him, she asked demurely, "How may I please you, Master?"

"Suck his dick while I tease you with the crop."

Brie bit her lip, even more turned on when she heard his command. Turning to face Rytsar, she leaned forward on her hands and knees to kiss his hard shaft.

"That's it, *radost moya*. Let me watch as you take my cock into your mouth."

Brie parted her pink lips and slowly encased the head of his shaft while she stared up at him, batting her eyes prettily—the picture of innocence.

She felt the erotically ticklish feel of the crop's leather tongue as Sir ran it up the length of one thigh and down the other. She felt its sting again as he slapped her buttocks with it.

Brie moaned on Rytsar's cock, her pussy already dripping with excitement.

"Take him deeper," Sir commanded.

Brie relaxed the muscles in her throat as the Russian fisted her hair and guided his rigid shaft into her mouth.

"*Krasivaya,*" Rytsar murmured while he watched her take him down her throat.

While she deep-throated him, Sir continued to play with the crop. He gently tapped the leather tongue across her back, before leaning forward to caress her breasts with the instrument. She felt the slippery hardness of his cock rubbing against her clit, and ached for him to claim her with it.

"It has been too long, *moy droog*," Rytsar groaned. "I have little restraint with her."

Brie loved hearing that Rytsar was struggling not to come in her mouth. Knowing she had the power to make the sadist crazy like that acted as an aphrodisiac, and she sucked even harder while increasing her rhythm.

Sir flicked the crop against her ass, knowing exactly what she was doing. "Slow and steady, téa."

Brie batted her eyes innocently at Rytsar as she pulled out momentarily and smiled up at him. Then she took him again inch by slow inch.

His low growl filled the room. "I can smell how wet her cunt is…"

"Would you like to feel it?" Sir asked.

"*Da*," he groaned. Changing positions, Rytsar lay on his back and ordered Brie to mount herself on his cock.

With help from Sir, she straddled Rytsar's waist and lowered herself. She hesitated for a moment when she felt the head of his cock press against her opening, wanting to tease him just a bit more.

Rytsar was having none of it and grabbed her waist with both hands, forcing her to take the entirety of his shaft. Brie cried out in exquisite pleasure, her body primed and ready to be fucked.

"Wait," Sir ordered, pressing her down on Rytsar's chest.

Brie remained still when she felt Sir move away from her. Soon, however, she heard the familiar sound of him coating his shaft with lubricant. "Although my cock is covered in your juices and I could take you now, you'll need the extra lubricant because I plan to fuck you deep and hard."

She shivered in delight, excited by the challenge of their double pounding. "Please, Master!"

The satisfying sound of his hand smacking her ass rang through the bedroom as he positioned himself behind her. "I will hold nothing back, téa."

Her pussy contracted with excitement at the thought, squeezing Rytsar's cock, making him groan in pleasurable frustration.

Sir positioned his cock against her tight rosette and slowly began to penetrate her. She whimpered softly, her body aching as she took his cock deep in her ass.

Brie was addicted to the challenge and relished the excitement of taking both men at the same time. There was no other feeling like it!

"Take her deep until you can take no more," Sir told Rytsar.

Rytsar grunted, tightening his grip around her waist. He smirked as he gazed into Brie's eyes. "I will show no mercy."

She moaned loudly in response, forcing herself to relax as both men soon matched each other's rhythm, thrusting into her with strokes that were deep and demanding.

When they ramped up the pace, she screamed with pleasure and pain, her eyelids fluttering as she completely let go and let them have their way with her body.

Flying on the sub-high their double penetration created, Brie encouraged them to fuck her even harder. Soon, the two men were grunting like animals as they gave her exactly what she asked for.

"Oh God, oh God…" Brie cried, her entire body tingling as she approached the edge of the pleasurable abyss.

Both men were relentless and did not let up. Finally, Rytsar roared like a beast as his body stiffened and he began releasing his seed deep inside her. Sir's climax followed immediately, and he fucked her ass hard as he came.

Feeling them orgasm inside her at the same time was exceedingly erotic and she screamed in passion to let them know how much she loved it.

When Sir finished, he disengaged and collapsed beside her, panting heavily while a satisfied smile spread across his face.

Rytsar let out a satisfied growl. "There is nothing like celebrating a near-death experience by fucking one's brains out."

"I agree, brother."

When Brie went to roll off Rytsar, he suddenly stopped her and commanded, "Stay."

Wrapping his arms around her, Rytsar began murmuring Russian words in her ear, confessing his deep and abiding love for her.

Then he looked up at the heavens and thanked God for sparing their lives. Turning to Sir, he demanded, "You must promise never to die, brother."

Sir chuckled.

"At the very least, wait until I am gone."

"I'll see what I can do."

"Good."

Brie sighed happily while she listened to their banter. She felt completely worn out and content. "This was exactly what my soul needed."

Clicking his tongue, Rytsar glanced at Sir. "Only one thing can make the moment better."

"What's that?"

"Vodka."

Brie giggled when Rytsar shouted, "Maxim, bring me a bottle and three shot glasses."

Moments later, Maxim came to the door with a tray.

Rytsar stood up in all his naked glory and took it from him.

Carrying the tray back to the bed, Rytsar set it on the nightstand and filled the three glasses.

He handed the first one to Brie. "A toast to mark the day you cheated death."

She took the glass from him, giggling softly when he handed her a pickle. "You know, I've never done a shot in bed."

Rytsar winked at her before handing the next glass to Sir. He took the last one for himself. Once he had rejoined them on the bed, he raised his glass to them.

"Here's to facing death and living to tell about it!"

As she clinked glasses with both men, Brie realized her experience that day had shown her what was most important in her life. It wasn't fame, riches, or even her beloved films. It was much simpler than that.

All Brie truly needed was Sir, her family, and the love of a certain Russian.

Nadia

After freshening up and donning the new clothes Rytsar had thoughtfully laid out for her, Brie followed the men out of the bedroom. She found Maxim on the floor with an abundance of toys, playing with Hope while gently rocking Anthony in his infant carrier.

Brie smiled, impressed. "Thank you, Maxim. You are a natural with my children."

The muscular bodyguard got up off the floor and straightened his suit before nodding to her.

Hope ran to Rytsar and raised her arms, wanting to be picked up. He happily obliged and kissed her on the forehead. "I can never hug you enough, *moye solntse.*"

"*Gospodin,*" Maxim said in a serious tone, "Barinov phoned and asked if they could move up the meeting today. He emphasized it is imperative for the project."

Rytsar frowned. "That does not bode well."

Looking at Sir and Brie, he explained, "There have been issues with the materials used for the containment facility we're building, and I can't risk having construction delayed."

"Agreed," Sir replied.

"Set the meeting in an hour, Maxim."

Looking at both of them, Rytsar offered, "You are certainly welcome to join me."

Brie glanced at Anthony, who was sleeping peacefully for now, but she knew he would be awake and hungry soon. "Why don't I stay behind with the children? If you need my input, you can always call me."

"Are you sure?" Sir asked.

She smiled confidently. "I am, Sir. Besides, I want a chance to talk to Faelan when he returns."

Brie gave Rytsar a worried look. "Do you think he'll be back soon?"

He shrugged. "The boy is known to walk the streets of Moskva-City for hours."

"Is that safe?"

"As long as Little Sparrow is with him, there is no reason to worry."

Rytsar then stared at Hope and the baby as if he was reluctant to leave them. But he suddenly seemed to have a flash of inspiration. "I have the perfect way to keep the three of you entertained while we are gone."

"What's that?" Brie asked.

He raised an eyebrow in answer. "You must wait to find out. Consider it payment—one good surprise deserves another."

"Just a little hint?" she begged.

"*Nyet,*" he said with finality, giving her a wicked grin. Handing Hope to her, he gave them both a kiss on the cheek before leaving with Sir and Maxim.

To pass the time while she waited for Faelan to return, Brie decided to explore the apartment with Hope. Opening the sliding glass doors to the indoor pool, Brie was once again awed by the white marble pillars surrounding the stylish pool, along with its black tile and the glass dome above. But, she was shocked to see that the entire pool had a childproof fence surrounding it now.

Rytsar had had no idea they would be coming, yet he had set this up in anticipation that they might visit. Rubbing noses with Hope, she told her daughter, "Your *dyadya* is a remarkable man. Too bad I didn't think to bring swimsuits on this trip."

After Brie left the pool area, she heard Anthony fussing and headed back. Setting Hope on the couch next to her, Brie unbuttoned her blouse. Anthony latched on hungrily and soon quieted.

Brie placed a blanket over her shoulder to cover him in case one of Rytsar's staff walked into the room. Then she lay back and relaxed.

She loved nursing because it forced her to live in the moment as she connected with her son on a soul level.

When she heard the front door open, Brie immediately sat up.

"Don't mind me," Faelan muttered, closing the door once Little Sparrow was inside. He picked up his pace as he headed down the hallway.

"Please, Faelan, can we talk?"

He paused for a moment and then turned back, but he avoided looking at her when he sat down on the couch. She noticed he chose to sit on the left side so his eyepatch would block any view of her.

"What do you want to talk about?"

"I'm sorry my being here upsets you," Brie told him.

"It's not you. It's just…" He sighed uncomfortably. "Seeing your baby hit me hard. I wasn't expecting it."

"I apologize that we came unannounced. Sir wanted to surprise Rytsar."

"He wasn't the only one you surprised," he chuckled ruefully.

Brie cut to the chase rather than pretend things were all right when she could clearly see they were not. "You don't seem well. I hoped coming to Russia with Rytsar would help you recover."

When he turned to face her, she saw the pain reflected in his blue eye. It was so intense, she had to look away.

"Kylie is still dead, Brie. Nothing has changed, other than my location." He glanced at Anthony briefly and frowned. "Your baby only reminds me of everything I've lost."

"But Grace needs you," Brie reminded him.

He shook his head. "You might think that, but you'd be wrong. I'm not fit to be a father, especially to an infant. They need care and attention, and I have nothing to give her. I can barely get through the day as it is. No child deserves to be neglected."

He stood up, crossing his arms. "The only thing of value I can give her is to protect her from Lilly. That is my sole purpose for living now."

"It doesn't have to be that way," she insisted.

"Trust me. The child is better off without me. I understand that now."

"You're wrong!" Brie cried. "She needs her daddy's love."

"Don't you get it? I have none to give her!" he shouted. His voice trailed off, and then he muttered, "I will only bring her pain…"

Hope whimpered when Faelan yelled at her mother and was desperately clutching onto Brie.

"See that?" he growled, pointing at Hope. "That's exactly what I'm talking about." He stormed down the hallway and slammed his door shut.

Brie hugged Hope, her heart breaking for Faelan. "He has a booboo, honey."

"Booboo?"

"Yes, sweet pea. He yells because it hurts," she explained. "He just needs someone to kiss it and make it better…"

While she finished burping Anthony, the doorbell rang. As if out of nowhere, one of the staff members appeared, walking briskly to the door the moment Brie stood up to answer it.

"Let me get that," the man insisted.

Brie was grateful to Rytsar's continued lessons, because the old woman at the door replied in Russian, "Anton asked me to come and entertain his guest."

"We have been expecting you," the man said warmly.

Brie walked to the door, curious who Rytsar had invited to surprise her.

Supported by a cane, the stout woman moved stiffly as she stepped into the apartment. Snow white hair peeked out from under the red scarf she wore around her head. The elderly woman looked like someone who'd survived hard times and had forgotten how to smile. But, the moment she saw the children, her whole face lit up and she cried, "*Mladentsy!*"

Slowly making her way to them, the woman's smile never faltered. Hope watched her approach and did not move when the old woman bent down to gently caress her cheek. "*Moye solntse*, you are as beautiful as Anton said."

The visitor then glanced at Anthony, who was squirming in Brie's arms as she tried to burp him.

"May I?"

Normally, Brie would have hesitated to hand her child to a stranger, but there was something about this woman that Brie trusted on a gut level. Taking him gently in her arms, the old woman pressed him against her ample breasts and began lightly rubbing his back. A few seconds later, Anthony let out a satisfying burp.

The old woman smiled at Brie. "I'd hoped this day would come. I have longed to see Rytsar's 'sunshine' and 'pride' with my own eyes."

Brie looked at her apologetically. "I'm sorry, but I don't know who you are."

The woman chuckled. "I am no one important."

Brie shook her head and grinned. "You must be to Rytsar."

She nodded thoughtfully. "I've known that boy since the day he was born."

"Are you related?" Brie asked excitedly.

She laughed. "Oh, no. I was just the cook."

Brie's jaw dropped. "Are you Nadia?"

She looked surprised. "You have heard of me?"

"You made that incredible cake for Rytsar's birthday."

Nadia's eyes twinkled when she said, "It was a true honor to make his mother's cake for Anton."

Brie couldn't help herself and threw her arms around Nadia. However, she immediately felt the woman stiffen. Quickly letting go, Brie stepped back and smiled. "It is wonderful to meet you in person. Rytsar speaks so highly of you."

The old woman blushed. "He exaggerates."

Brie grinned and gestured toward the couch. "Please, sit down."

Shaking her head, Nadia told her, "We have a cake to bake."

Brie stared at her as tears came to her eyes. "You're going to show me how to bake Mamulya's cake?"

Nadia patted her cheek tenderly. "It's the reason I came, Brianna."

While she slowly made her way to the kitchen, Brie saw that Rytsar's staff was busy getting out all of the ingredients and a special stool for Nadia, so she could sit comfortably at the counter while she baked.

Brie hefted Hope up and sat her on the counter beside them so she could watch Nadia bake the honey cake. She then rushed off and pulled out a baby sling from her suitcase so Anthony could be in the middle of the action as well.

For the next few hours, Brie watched with rapt attention as Nadia showed her each step to make the perfect Medovic cake. Although the ingredients themselves were simple, Brie quickly realized it was the time and love put into each thin layer of the cake that truly made it exceptional.

"It must be thin and uniform," Nadia insisted.

Brie practiced over and over before she earned Nadia's approval. She took the task seriously, thrilled to be learning Mamulya's recipe through someone who knew her.

By the time they were done, Brie was covered in flour and icing. But, with Nadia's careful instruction, she'd made a truly beautiful cake.

"I can't wait for Rytsar to try this!" Brie gushed.

"And he will. Tomorrow," Nadia replied.

Brie had to hide her disappointment. "That's right. I forgot it has to rest for a day."

"You cannot rush perfection, Brianna," she stated, placing the glass dome over the cake to protect it. "Now, put it in the fridge and give it the time it needs."

Brie reverently picked up the cake and carried it to the refrigerator. "Will you return tomorrow to taste it with us?"

The old woman laughed as she shook her head. "It will take me a least a day to recover from baking."

Brie frowned in concern. "I'm so sorry."

"Don't be. There is nothing on Earth I would rather do than pass the recipe for this cake on to you. It was a dream come true."

"It was for me, too!" Brie agreed.

"Now I must return to my bed," Nadia stated matter-of-factly.

Brie helped her off the stool and two of Rytsar's men instantly appeared to escort her home.

"I can't thank you enough for today," Brie told her. "It is a gift I will never forget."

Wanting to give her something in return, Brie grabbed her phone and handed it to one of the men. "Can you please take a picture of the four of us?"

The man nodded, holding up the camera while Brie took Anthony out of the sling and handed him to Nadia. Picking up Hope, Brie sang out, "Smile at the camera, sweet pea!" as she wrapped an arm around Nadia. Rather than stiffen as before, Nadia relaxed in Brie's embrace.

"I will send you this picture to commemorate this day," she promised.

Nadia turned and surprised Brie by kissing her on the cheek. "It has been lovely getting to spend time with the woman who saved Anton."

Brie shook her head, smiling, "I didn't save him."

The old woman's eyes twinkled when she said, "Your love did."

"So did yours, Nadia."

Slice of Heaven

The next day, at the appointed time, Rytsar insisted everyone, including his staff, gather at the dining room table so he could take the first bite of the Medovik cake.

Brie was both honored and nervous. She was worried it might not live up to Mamulya's standards, even with Nadia's help.

Faelan sat in a chair at the far end of the table, looking disinterested as he petted Little Shadow's head.

"Bring in the cake!" Rytsar announced.

Taking a deep breath, Brie picked up the large crystal cake stand and slowly made her way to the table. Setting it down with Sir's help, she carefully lifted the glass dome with a flourish.

Hope clapped in excitement. Surprising everyone, she suddenly climbed onto the table and made a beeline for the cake. Sir saved the day by deftly swooping her up in his arms. "Let your *dyadya* cut the cake first, little angel."

Several of the staff snickered under their breath.

Rytsar, eyeing the cake critically, slowly spun the cake plate around, looking at it from every angle. Brie smiled hesitantly when he nodded in satisfaction.

Picking up a silver knife, he sliced through the cake. "It has the proper firmness through each layer," he stated. After cutting a single piece, he lifted up the plate to examine the layers.

Brie cheered silently when she saw how beautiful the layers were, each one sandwiched between the perfect amount of icing.

"Stunning," Rytsar stated. "But the true test is in the taste."

Brie held her breath as she watched him slice through the piece with his fork and put it up to his lips. He winked at her before opening his mouth and taking the bite.

Closing his eyes, Rytsar chewed slowly. The expression on his face remained neutral, so she couldn't tell whether he cared for it or not.

When he finally opened his eyes, his stern gaze landed on her. "*Radost moya.*"

"Yes, Rytsar?" she squeaked.

"*Mamulya* would be proud."

Brie let out a sigh of relief. She was touched when the staff applauded.

Handing the knife to her, Rytsar commanded, "I want you to cut a piece for every person here."

She counted the number of people and looked at the cake to determine the size of each slice.

Brie's hand shook with excitement as she cut the

cake. Knowing that she had successfully re-created a beloved dish for Rytsar had her riding on an emotional high.

After doling out cake to everyone, Brie stood back and waited eagerly for everyone to taste it.

"Haven't you forgotten someone?" Sir asked her.

She looked around to make sure everyone had a piece. "I don't think so."

He smiled. "Where is your piece?"

Brie blushed, giggling, "I was too excited."

Rytsar pulled his seat back, patting his lap. "Come sit, and I will share my piece with you."

Brie walked up to him and smiled as she sat down on his muscular lap. Cutting another bite of the cake with his fork, he instructed everyone to eat, exclaiming warmly, "Taste my childhood!"

Rytsar's movements were slow and sensual as he brought the fork up to her parted lips…then quickly took the bite himself. She burst out laughing and watched as Sir gave a small bite to Hope. After tasting it, Hope's eyes widened. Instead of taking the next bite Sir offered her, she reached out and grabbed a big handful of his cake, stuffing it in her mouth.

Rytsar roared. "*Moye solntse*, I could not love you more!"

Picking up his own piece of cake with his hand, Rytsar brought it to Brie's lips. She looked at him warily. "You're not going to smash it in my face, are you?"

Rytsar raised an eyebrow and ordered, "Open."

Brie obeyed but silently expected to get a face full of cake. Instead, he held it still and, as she took a bite, murmured in her ear, "I will never forget this gift of love, *radost moya*."

Tears of joy ran down her face as the delicious flavors and textures of the honey cake melded in her mouth. Truly, it was the best cake she had ever tasted.

"I feel her spirit here," Rytsar confessed to her.

Brie swallowed down the lump in her throat, touched by his confession, and nodded.

Once he took the last bite of the cake, Rytsar licked his fingers and then asked Faelan, "Why haven't you taken a bite?"

He shrugged. "I'm not hungry."

Rytsar scoffed. "It is rude not to eat a dish when it has been made with love."

Faelan glanced at Brie and picked up his fork. He took a small bite with everyone watching and shrugged. "It's good."

"Good?" Rytsar protested. "It is a taste of heaven. Take another bite."

To humor the sadist, Faelan took a larger bite and chewed it more slowly, before swallowing.

"Well?" Rytsar demanded.

There was a catch in Faelan's voice when he answered, "There *is* a bit of heaven in this cake."

Rytsar pounded the table. "*Da!*"

He then ordered, "Maxim, get glasses for everyone!"

A flurry of activity followed as glasses were handed out and vodka poured.

Brie barely heard the cell phone ringing in Faelan's pocket but caught the look on his face when he answered it.

A cold chill ran down her spine.

Jumping off Rytsar's lap, she glanced at Sir in concern. He nodded in Faelan's direction, gesturing for her to go to him.

Brie followed as Faelan walked down the hallway and, as she drew near, she heard him sigh. "I don't know… Hell, maybe they should." He glanced up and noticed Brie standing there. "Look, I don't have an answer for you right now." He paused for a moment, then snarled, "I'll have to think about it and call you back!"

He wore a numb expression when he hung up the phone and slipped it back into his pocket.

"Is everything okay?" Brie asked gently.

"I don't know…" He shook his head and started down the hallway, heading for his room.

Brie quietly followed, her concern for him growing with each step. When he got to his room, he walked to the bed and sat down, burying his face in his hands.

Leaning against the doorway, she prodded in a soft voice, "Who was that on the phone?"

Not looking up, he answered, "Asher."

Brie immediately felt a sense of foreboding. "What did Marquis Gray say to you?"

Faelan let out a ragged sigh. Glancing up, he ordered, "Come in and shut the door."

With her heart racing, Brie closed the door, shutting out the sounds of laughter coming from the dining room.

She stood by the door, afraid of what he would say.

"It seems Kylie's parents are suing for custody of the baby."

"No!"

Faelan turned his head to her, his voice void of emotion. "Maybe I should let them have her."

Brie rushed to his side. "Don't say that! I'm sure they mean well, but the best place for your daughter is with her daddy."

Faelan frowned. "They've raised a child before and did a damn good job of it. Maybe it's for the best."

Brie knelt, taking his hands in hers. "Don't think about yourself right now. Think about Kylie. What would Kylie want for her daughter?"

Faelan shook his head. "It doesn't matter."

Squeezing his hands tighter, Brie said, "You love Kylie with all of your heart. I know you care…"

A sob escaped his lips.

"You're not alone," she encouraged him. "It takes a village to raise a child, and you have a whole army."

"Oh, Brie…" he said in a defeated voice. "You have no idea what I can or can't do."

She looked him dead in the eye. "I know Kylie believed in you just as much as I do."

Her words seemed to set him off. He pushed away from her and stood up, walking to the other side of the room. "I hate you for saying that."

"Why? Because it's true? Instead of fighting it, embrace her belief in you. She never left. She's right here. Can't you feel it?"

Faelan looked up to the heavens and ripped off his eyepatch. He howled in pain, "Yes, I feel her…damn it! I felt her love when I tasted your fucking cake. But it only makes it worse. Don't you get that? She is like a whisper

I can barely hear, and it's not enough. I want to hold her, to make love to her, and fall asleep in her arms every night…"

He turned to face her with a look of desperation. "Every day is torture without her."

Brie swallowed hard as the depth of his pain washed over her.

"I am living in a black abyss and anyone who gets too close will fall into it with me."

She knew he was too distraught to believe in a future without Kylie in it. "Don't give up, Faelan. Keep fighting for Kylie's sake and your baby."

He winced, looking at her as if she had just struck him. "Get the fuck out of here, Brie. Leave me alone!"

She headed to the door. The moment she opened it, the sound of laughter drifted into the room. As she slowly shut the door behind her, she told him, "Kylie wants to hear you laugh again."

The sound of a boot crashing into the door echoed down the hallway as she walked away.

Brie tossed and turned that night, struggling to sleep. Concerned she might wake Sir, she slipped out of bed and left the room, closing the door behind her.

As she tiptoed down the hallway, she heard male voices ahead. Naturally curious, she stayed out of sight as she snuck up, wanting to hear what they were talking about.

Faelan's ragged voice filled the air when he asked, "Do you ever feel like God hates you?"

The rumble of Rytsar's low chuckle made Brie smile. "*Nyet*. If God hated me, I would not have been raised by an incredible woman or known the love of a soulmate."

"But you lost them both."

"*Da*, I have known great pain," he agreed. "However, I have also experienced unspeakable joy. Life is not one or the other but a mixture of both."

"I don't see the point of living if that's the case."

"How can you say that when you willingly sacrificed your eye so I could live?" Rytsar demanded.

"You had something to live for…people who cared about you."

"Are you blind?"

He frowned. "You have someone who loves you and who you can love back."

"Do you mean *radost moya*?"

"Of course…" he replied defensively.

Rytsar chuckled. "I met her over eighteen years after Tatianna died. Had I given up, I would never have known that extraordinary woman or been *dyadya* to her children."

Brie blushed in response.

"No one can predict the future," he told Faelan. "But, as a man who has lived through the depths of hell, I tell you it will be worth the journey."

"I don't believe you," Faelan growled dismissively.

"I'm restraining myself from punching you right now because I owe you my life. But I am more stubborn than you, and will *not* let you give up."

"You are making me regret saving you," Faelan snarled.

The Russian suddenly burst out laughing. "Be as surly as you want, I can handle it. But know this—there is a version of yourself waiting in the future to toast you for all the pain you've overcome."

Brie put her hands to her heart, deeply moved by his words.

"Fuck you, Durov!" Faelan snarled.

She heard him get up and start walking in her direction. She scampered on light feet down the hallway, disappearing into the bedroom before he even knew she was there.

Her heart beating like a drum, she held her breath as he walked past. It wasn't until she heard his door shut that she finally let out her breath.

Her stomach jumped when she heard Sir's voice behind her.

"You have some explaining to do, babygirl."

Confronting the Past

After Sir ordered Brie to come back to bed, she explained what she had heard. Although she could not fathom how Faelan could even consider giving up custody of his daughter, Sir was more sympathetic to his situation.

"Babygirl, you know I also questioned my ability to be a fit parent. It speaks to his deep concern for her."

"But she *needs* him!" Brie insisted.

"It's a decision he must make on his own. Forcing the issue won't benefit either him or the child. In fact, it could make things worse. We both know he is not emotionally stable right now."

Brie understood what Sir was saying, but it gutted her to think of baby Grace being separated from her father. "It doesn't feel right!"

Sir wrapped his arm around her. "Durov has given him good counsel tonight, and I am certain Marquis is doing the same."

"What if it isn't enough?" she whimpered.

"Patience, my love. He needs time to think this through." He kissed her lightly on the lips. "Now, try to get some rest. We have a long day tomorrow."

Brie snuggled against Sir and closed her eyes. She tried to sleep, but she was haunted by the sound of Grace crying the day Faelan left her.

Please Faelan, Brie begged silently, *you have to find the strength.*

Since Brie was in Russia, she felt it was important to see Lilly in person while she was there. Rytsar had made arrangements for the four of them to travel but, while packing for the three-day trip, Faelan knocked on the doorframe of their guestroom and informed them, "I wanted to tell you I'm not going. I have zero interest in making a trek to see Lilly."

"You have to come," Brie insisted, worried about him being alone.

"I've already discussed it with Durov, and he agrees my time would be better spent staying here to oversee the construction project while he is gone. *Someone* has to make sure those materials arrive in time."

"I sincerely regret you won't be joining us," Sir stated. If he was concerned about Faelan staying behind, Brie saw no evidence of it.

Sweeping his fingers through his hair, Faelan laughed, "You're in for some freaky shit."

"What do you mean?" Brie asked him.

He shook his head. "That's something Durov has to tell you himself."

It was obvious Faelan had no interest in talking about the custody issue because he immediately headed to his bedroom and shut the door.

Brie turned to Sir. "Do you have any clue what he means by freaky shit?"

"No, but I aim to find out."

Brie followed close behind as Sir went to search for Rytsar. They found the Russian reading a book on the couch.

Sir demanded, "Is there something you aren't telling us?"

Rytsar glanced up from his book, looking unconcerned. "Everything has been arranged. There is no need for concern. Normally, I would fly, but we will be taking the train."

He then glanced in the direction of Faelan's bedroom, adding in a lower voice, "For obvious reasons he can't know about."

Brie realized Rytsar was ensuring Faelan remained in the dark about their near-crash.

"That is thoughtful of you," Sir replied, glancing at Brie. "I don't think either of us is prepared to fly quite yet."

Brie involuntarily shuddered.

"We'll be heading out soon, but before we leave, I've made an appointment with an esthetician for you," Rytsar informed Brie. "With your Master's permission, of course. She will be here within the hour to give you a thorough waxing."

"Why?" she asked, looking at both men, curious what Rytsar had planned.

"It will be made clear soon enough, *radost moya*," the Russian stated, hinting to nothing more.

Although Brie was intrigued, she was still concerned about Faelan. "Do you think it's safe to leave Faelan alone right now?"

"Absolutely," Rytsar replied. "My staff is aware of his situation, and Little Sparrow watches him like a hawk. If anything is amiss, she'll let them know."

Brie felt a flood of relief. "I feel much better knowing that."

"I will not let that boy down, *radost moya*. Did I not promise you that?"

She smiled sheepishly. "You did."

"I *never* break my promises."

Brie was instantly reminded of how he kept his promise to Hope when he was kidnapped by the Koslov brothers. "I will never doubt you again, Rytsar."

"See that you don't," he commanded gently.

When they arrived at the train station, Brie was surprised to see that Rytsar had reserved the luxurious end car for them. Not only that, but he had hired a private chef and a nanny to help with the children during the trip.

"Talk about living the high life!" Brie exclaimed as she boarded the train. The long car was decorated with plush red velvet seats, extravagant window treatments, a formal dining table, and gold accents scattered tastefully throughout. "I feel like royalty."

"You should be treated like a queen." Rytsar took her hand and kissed it.

Deeply touched, she looked into his intense blue eyes. "It's an honor to love you, Anton Durov."

His lips twitched and he leaned in, whispering in a seductive voice, "Remember that when I have you bent over, screaming out in glorious pain as I drill you with my cock."

Brie bit her lip, her pussy instantly aching in response to his words.

As the train pulled out, Rytsar took a photo from his pocket and handed it to Sir. "Do you remember this, brother?"

Sir stared at the picture, a smile playing across his lips. He then handed it to Brie. "I do, as a matter of fact."

The photo was of a cave splashed with intense colors of yellows, oranges, and reds. "Who painted this?" she asked.

"God," Rytsar answered simply.

"Are you saying this is natural?" she questioned, looking at the photo again.

"*Da.* Your Master and I had a date to go there a long time ago, but fate had other plans for us…" He glanced at Sir.

Brie sat up, realizing she was about to learn something new about their past. "What happened?"

Sir scoffed. "I can't believe you are taking us there—and on a train, no less." Looking at Rytsar in concern, he added, "I'd rather not."

Rytsar grasped his shoulder. "I have longed to see this ever since I was a boy. You know this."

"Yes, I do. But, a train, Durov? Why spare us the torture, only to put yourself through it?"

"It is time, brother," he insisted.

Brie had no clue what they were talking about and was desperate to find out. "What happened on the train?"

"We never made it to the salt mine, babygirl." Sir's gaze never left Rytsar when he explained, "The train was hit by a freak avalanche."

Brie felt chills. "Was anyone hurt?"

"Many did not survive, including two of my men," Rytsar answered her, the pain of grief coloring his voice.

Brie's heart ached for him. "I'm so sorry to hear that."

Shaking it off, Rytsar stated, "That is in the past. I am about to make new memories that will replace the old, with the people I hold most dear."

He swooped Hope up into his arms and walked with her to a large box tied with a red bow. "I saw you eyeing this gift, *moye solntse*, and you are right. It is for you and your baby brother."

The moment he set the gift down, Hope tore the bow off. With a little help from her *dyadya*, Hope ripped off the paper and lifted the lid of the box. She squealed when she saw the inside was filled with hundreds of colorful bows cushioning the toys inside.

True to form, their little girl went for the bows first, grabbing a handful and scattering them on the floor.

Playing with the plentiful bows was as entertaining for her as the actual presents, which made Rytsar smile. When Hope finally pulled out a plushy with a pacifier attached, he told her, "That is for Anthony."

"Antony?" she asked. When he nodded, Hope toddled over to her baby brother and placed it near him, running back to get another toy.

"I like the way she pronounces his name," Rytsar stated with a smirk as he stood up.

Brie wrapped an arm around Sir. "We do, too."

"In fact, we are considering permanently calling him by Hope's nickname," Sir informed him.

Rytsar stared at them with an expression Brie could not read and she asked, "Would that be all right with you?"

"*Da*," he replied, his voice gruff with emotion.

While the train ride was lavish and uneventful, there came a point when Brie felt waves of tension emanating from Rytsar. He walked to a window and watched the snowy scenery speed past as they climbed the side of a steep mountain.

"Are we getting close?" Sir asked him.

"*Da*," he replied.

Walking over to him, Sir placed his hand on his shoulder. "We had no idea what we were heading into that night."

Rytsar nodded. "I will forever be indebted to you,

moy droog."

"No need. I did it for purely selfish reasons, old friend."

Rytsar snorted.

Brie had no idea what the two of them were referencing, but she wrapped her arms around Rytsar in support. After several minutes, she noticed his anxiety increase tenfold.

"We are almost there," he announced, kissing Brie on the top of the head.

Breaking away from her, Rytsar headed to the door at the end of the car which opened onto a small outdoor balcony. The icy chill of the fresh mountain air rushed into the car, causing Brie to shiver as she watched, transfixed, as Rytsar raised his hands wide and looked up to the heavens.

"I survived!" he roared at the top of his lungs. The sound of his cry echoed several times through the mountain valley.

Brie swallowed the lump that had formed in her throat, moved by the power behind his cry.

Rytsar nodded several times as he scanned the mountainous terrain, then walked back inside, sliding the door closed. Brie sensed a much more confident aura around him that hadn't been there when they first boarded the train. It took her breath away.

"Damn, it feels good to be alive!" he shouted, the spark in his eyes captivating. Walking up to Sir, he grabbed him in a manly embrace. "It was important for me to share this moment with you, brother."

Sir slapped him on the back. "Can't believe we survived to tell about it."

"We have all cheated death, isn't it a glorious feeling?" Rytsar took in a deep breath, letting it out slowly, a look of satisfaction on his face. "That night, when I was buried under the snow and thought all was lost, I had no idea what the future had in store for me—or the extraordinary people I would come to know and love."

His gaze fell on Brie and the two children. "I am truly a blessed man."

Rubbing his hands together excitedly, Rytsar then declared, "And now for the salt mines of Yekaterinburg. The only way to access the caverns is by a government permit, which I have procured. My childhood dream is about to become an adult fantasy!"

Sir raised an eyebrow. "What exactly do you have planned?"

"A night of debauchery inside the caverns, *moy droog*."

Brie laughed. "What about the children?"

"That's what the nanny is for."

"Ahh…" she said, standing on her tiptoes to give him a kiss. "Now, I'm even more excited to fulfill this childhood dream of yours."

Hours later, as they walked up to the entrance to the salt mine, Brie noticed a man waiting for them.

"Is everything prepared?" Rytsar asked.

"Yes, *gospodin*. To your exact specifications."

"Excellent. I do not expect to return until morning."

"Understood." He handed them each a helmet with a headlamp.

Brie noticed there were also hiking boots and canteens of water for each of them.

Sir took Brie's helmet from her and placed it on her head, securing the strap under her chin. "Are you okay, babygirl?"

Brie was amazed that Sir had picked up on her growing anxiety. Although she had never mentioned it, she'd been afraid of dark, confined spaces since she was a child. So, the idea of exploring a cave was a tad frightening to her, but she refused to miss this experience because of those fears.

"I'm nervous but excited," she answered truthfully.

Sir lifted her chin, kissing her tenderly on the lips. "Know that I would never let anything happen to you."

Brie gazed into his eyes and lost herself for a moment when he kissed her again.

"There will be time enough for *that*," Rytsar joked. It was obvious by the tone of his voice that he was anxious to start exploring the cave.

Holding on tight to Sir's hand, Brie turned on her headlamp. With her heart beating like a drum, she followed Rytsar into the dark cavern.

Masterpiece

A s they made their way into the darkness, Rytsar began sharing interesting facts about the Salt Mine of Yekaterinburg.

"The magnificent art that decorates the cave walls is made up of layers of a mineral called carnallite that appears in a variety of different colors. These deposits date back to 280 million years ago, when an entire sea dried up, leaving a salty residue of evaporated minerals."

Rytsar led them to a metal cage. "Tonight, we will be traveling 650 feet below the surface in this hoist."

Brie swallowed hard when she entered the steel contraption covered in splotches of salt layers. Her anxiety only increased when Rytsar slid the door closed and locked it.

Her heart raced the moment he pressed a green button and the hoist jerked to life. The butterflies in her stomach started when she looked through the cage bars. The roughly hewn stone sped by as they descended deep under the ground. She could even feel the temperature drop the lower they went.

"We are traveling six hundred feet a minute. It won't take long," Rytsar chuckled.

The hoist began to slow before finally coming to a stop. Rytsar unlocked the door, and it creaked loudly as he slid it open.

"You get to be the first, *radost moya!*"

Brie understood Rytsar meant it as an honor, but she glanced nervously at Sir, squeezing his hand before stepping into the darkness. Her beam of light only revealed a small section of the cavern in front of her.

When she looked up, she couldn't believe how incredibly large the cave was.

Rytsar stepped up behind her. "The winding tunnels stretch for miles, some go longer than four miles."

"A person could easily get lost in here…" Brie muttered.

"Stick by me and you have nothing to fear," Rytsar assured her.

Their footsteps echoed through the dark cavern while he led them along as if he knew the path to take by heart. Brie wondered if he had studied the mine as a child, dreaming about coming here someday. Knowing that made her appreciate how important this was to him and bolstered her courage.

While they walked, Brie noticed the air seemed to taste of salt, leaving her mouth somewhat dry. She was grateful for the canteen as she opened it and took a long drink.

"Although the patterns of the mineral deposits are stunning, the colors are muted because of the limited light coming from these damn headlamps," Sir grumbled.

"Patience, *moy droog.*"

Brie experienced a sense of exhilarating danger, knowing they were the only ones down here exploring the silent cavern while people went about their everyday lives above.

"This way," Rytsar told them, the pitch of his voice rising with his excitement. He turned right and headed down a new tunnel.

Sir must have sensed her rising anxiety because he squeezed her hand tighter as they followed him deeper into the darkness. But, she could tell Sir was as excited as Rytsar, and that the allure of the unknown was calling to him like a siren song.

As Rytsar increased his pace, taking them farther from the safety of the hoist, Brie clung to his excitement to quell her own growing fears.

It reminded her of edge play, where she would explore her boundaries and see just how far she could push herself before finally calling out her safeword. She was almost at that point now.

Rytsar called out ahead of them, "This is it!"

Turning around to face them, he turned off his headlamp and held out his hand to Brie. "Shut off the light and follow the sound of my voice, *radost moya.* I want you to experience this moment properly."

Was she brave enough to obey Rytsar?

The butterflies in her stomach increased as she and Sir turned off their lights. The pitch-black darkness seemed to envelop her.

Swallowing hard, she let go of Sir's hand and called out, "Rytsar?"

"I'm right here," he answered.

She started forward, the pounding in her chest growing louder with each step. She wondered if they could hear it. The moment she hesitated to take the next step, he called out, "Come to me, *radost moya.*"

The warmth in his voice cut through the chill of the air, and she walked toward him confidently. "I'm coming…"

"*Da*, you will soon enough."

Brie smiled, but the dark was all-encompassing. Out of fear, she ran the last few steps, crashing into his chest before she felt his strong arms wrapping around her.

"Good girl."

Hearing Rytsar's praise, while locked in his powerful embrace, blocked out all fear.

"And now for your reward…" Suddenly, the cavern around them burst with warm light. Once her eyes adjusted Brie let out a gasp as she looked at the incredible beauty around her.

Brilliant colors of electric blue, yellow, red, and orange swirled around her in patterns that reminded her of animated gusts of wind. It was fantastic and utterly unreal.

"Extraordinary," Sir murmured in stunned awe.

Rytsar sighed in satisfaction. "I always knew it would feel like this…"

"Like what?" Brie asked breathlessly.

"Like I was standing beside God, witnessing a masterpiece only His immense creativity and patience could create."

Tears pricked her eyes when she heard his answer.

"It does feel like hallowed ground," Sir stated.

Rytsar's eyes flashed as he stared down at the scars on his wrist, "If I had to do it over again, brother, I would have performed our ritual here—the most sacred place on this planet."

Sir slowly scanned the area above them, a look of wonder on his face. "While I agree this would have been the perfect place…" He met Rytsar's gaze, before adding, "…the truth is it didn't matter where the ritual was performed. The only thing of consequence was the fidelity behind our vow to one another."

Rytsar nodded. "True enough, *moy droog.*"

The Russian then took Brie's wrist and turned it, looking tenderly at her scar. "The same is true for you and me."

She grazed her finger over the higher of the two scars on his wrist. "This meant more to me than you can know, Rytsar. You carried me through a very dark time."

"As did you, *radost moya.*"

Stepping away from them both, Rytsar raised his arms wide. "Now, the three of us will consecrate this hallowed place. Look behind you."

Brie turned and gasped in surprise. The floor of the cavern was covered in satin bedding with a multitude of colorful pillows artfully strewn about. Large pillar candles surrounded the area, giving it a decidedly romantic feel.

Rytsar meticulously lit each one, then lit the fuel canisters under a golden chafing dish.

Pointing to it, she asked, "What's that for?"

"Strip and I will show you," he commanded with a wicked grin.

"It's freezing," she protested, hoping he wasn't serious.

"It is a balmy seventy degrees in the salt mine, *radost moya.*"

"Balmy?" she giggled.

"Trust me. You won't feel the cold. Now, strip for your Master before I spank that cheeky ass." His Russian accent, along with his commanding tone, made her pussy drip with anticipation.

Brie obediently turned her attention on Sir.

Taking off her helmet first, she laid it on the ground, setting her canteen and hiking boots beside it. Brie then began moving in slow, measured movements as she undressed in front of Sir, wanting to seduce her Master as she exposed her body to him.

He stood before her, observing her every move. She felt the heat of his gaze as she undid her bra and let it fall to the floor. The cool air on her nipples instantly made them hard, which turned her on even more.

Maybe being cold isn't such a bad thing, she mused as goosebumps of excitement rose on her skin.

Once she had shimmied off her panties and stood completely naked before him, Sir commanded, "Turn for me."

He took out his phone and began taking pictures. Brie smiled at him alluringly as she slowly turned in place. The moment was elevated tenfold by the breathtaking art that surrounded her on all sides.

"Stunning," he murmured as he continued to photograph her.

"I agree, *moy droog*," Rytsar replied lustfully. "She looks good enough to eat."

"She does," Sir agreed, slipping his phone back in his pocket. "Shall we partake of her?"

"*Da*," he answered in a low growl.

Brie's heart began racing as Rytsar approached. Something about the man was feral, enticing, and equally frightening. Taking her wrist, he led her to the center of the bedding and ordered, "Kneel."

She gracefully knelt on the soft, satiny material.

Rytsar opened the chafing dish, revealing paint jars filled with vibrant colors. Picking up one of the jars, he swirled it several times, testing its viscosity. He seemed pleased. Taking one of the paintbrushes from another jar, he dipped the brush into the electric blue paint and then walked to Brie, grazing the wet brush over her lips.

"Taste," he ordered.

Brie licked the warm liquid from her lips and smiled when she tasted its familiar sweetness. "Chocolate."

His eyes burned with desire when he replied, "*Da.*"

Rytsar glanced at Sir. "What do you say we paint our own masterpiece, tonight?"

Sir smiled. "That is a truly inspired idea."

"First, I will take care of her hair while you freshen up her skin," Rytsar stated, pointing to a sponge and thermos.

Sir picked up both items and began the sensual process of thoroughly cleaning her body with the warm, soapy water. It was incredibly erotic when paired with the chill of the water evaporating on her skin. The contrasting sensations heightened the thrill of the experience.

While he cleaned her, Rytsar took an unused paintbrush and used the end of it to divide her hair into long strands that fanned out, framing her face with her long locks.

Once he was satisfied, Rytsar looked down at her and smiled. "No matter what we do, you must not move once we begin."

Brie smiled, exhilarated by the sexy challenge. "Yes, Rytsar."

Channeling her experience with objectification, Brie readied herself, staring up at the inspiring scenery above her. She never imagined that such beauty existed so deep underground.

"You begin with her feet, while I start on her face, *moy droog.*"

While Sir got comfortable, taking off his boots and grabbing a pillow to lean against, Rytsar picked up a remote and pressed a button. Suddenly, the cavern was filled with the sound of Alonzo's violin.

The combination of Alonzo's music and this hallowed place was sublime.

"Brother…" Sir said in a hoarse voice, obviously moved by Rytsar's choice of music. The two men looked at each other, an unspoken understanding passing between them.

As Brie lay there, listening to the haunting beauty of the violin, Sir began painting her feet with the warm chocolate. Brie struggled not to move when she felt the light, unbearably ticklish paint strokes across her sensitive toes.

Rytsar picked up one of the jars of colored chocolate and studied the wall for a moment before gliding the soft brush over her cheek. Her skin tingled wherever he touched her, making tears spring to her eyes. She had to will herself not to squirm.

The two men spent hours recreating the spectacular patterns and colors on the contours of her body. Brie experienced a unique sub-high as she gave in to the fragrant warmth of the chocolate and the light strokes of their brushes.

When they were done, both men stood up to admire their work. Rytsar clasped Sir's shoulder as he looked down at her proudly, "Truly a masterpiece."

Sir took out his phone and told Brie, "Look at me, téa. Embrace the fact you are a true goddess."

She was bursting with love for him as he snapped picture after picture of her. This moment would stand out as one of the most incredible experiences of her life—or so she thought until Rytsar announced, "And now we partake of our labors."

Both men undressed in front of her, exposing their intense desire for her. Sir then settled down at her feet while Rytsar positioned himself next to her head.

That's when she experienced erotic nirvana as the two men began licking the chocolate from her skin. Brie's eyes rolled into the back of her head as she gave in to the demanding heat of their tongues and the pressure of their teeth.

Brie trembled with anticipation when Sir began nibbling up her inner thigh, heading straight for her pussy, while Rytsar's tongue swirled around her erect nipple.

The men timed it perfectly, Sir's tongue teasing her clit as Rytsar encased her nipple with his lips and began sucking.

Brie cried out. She had no control as her breast released its milk into his mouth. Shuddering in pure ecstasy, she experienced a unique orgasm like no other.

Sir growled between her legs. "I love tasting your sweet come." His tongue showed her no mercy as he teased her clit.

Rytsar was equally merciless as he moved to her other breast and sucked it even harder.

Brie completely lost herself, flying on the sensual wave of pleasure the two men were skillfully creating. She had no idea how many times she came, the orgasms following one after the other.

When the men had reached their breaking point, Sir slammed his cock into her wet pussy while Rytsar claimed her throat with his cock. In a moment of erotic solidarity, the three of them climaxed together, filling the cavern with their sexual song.

Freaky Flower

They returned to the surface just in time to see the sunrise. After spending the night underground, watching the spectacular colors of the sunrise stretching over the icy terrain was like watching a miracle.

Brie turned to Rytsar, "I feel like I'm seeing a sunrise for the first time."

He placed his hand on the back of her neck and squeezed, making her feel like a helpless kitten in the best possible way. "I agree, *radost moya*. It's the beginning of a new season in our three lives."

Brie felt the truth of his statement in the depth of her soul and turned to Sir. "I can't wait to see what the future has in store for us."

He wrapped his arm around her waist while Rytsar held on to her. "With a new baby and the documentary coming out next summer, you have your hands full, babygirl."

She looked up at him and smiled. "I can accomplish anything with you by my side."

Rytsar cleared his throat. "That reminds me. You said once that you were looking for a house in Russia, *moy droog.*"

Chuckling, Sir explained, "We were, but life got in the way."

"Don't let that stop you. Your children will benefit from time spent in the motherland. Trust me."

Brie could imagine coming up each summer to spend time with Rytsar and having the children immersed in the language and traditions of the Russian people. It would be a beautiful way for him to pass those things he held dear onto their children in a real and meaningful way.

"We'll keep looking no matter how busy life gets," she promised.

"Good," Rytsar stated, nodding as they watched the sun break over the horizon.

Continuing by train, they made it to their final stop.

Brie was told it was a long, cold trek to the isolated convent, so she was tickled when she stepped off the train and saw a sleigh drawn by two horses waiting.

"Oh, my goodness! I've always wanted to ride on a sleigh! Do you see that, Hope? We're going to be riding on that sleigh."

Brie took Hope to pet the horses.

Sir joined them soon after, stating emphatically, "Hope will not be joining us, Brie."

"Why not? It should be fun."

Hope laughed joyously as she petted the horse's furry cheek.

"I do not want my children anywhere near Lilly. After what she did to you and Hope, I refused to take any more risks. She will remain here with the nanny."

"Funny you should say that, *moy droog*," Rytsar said, walking up to them. "I felt the same and made alternate arrangements for the children."

"Good," Sir replied curtly. "Let's get on our way and get this over with as soon as possible."

Brie could hear the tension in Sir's voice. Although he'd agreed Brie should see Lilly, it was obvious this trip was going to be extremely difficult for him. Brie knew he felt partially responsible for Lilly's actions because it was his half-sister who tried to hurt the baby while Brie was still carrying her. Lilly was also responsible for the two of them being kidnapped. If it hadn't been for the quick actions of Rytsar and Sir, both she and Hope would have become another tragic statistic in the dark underworld of sex trafficking.

Kissing Hope on the head, Sir handed her to the nanny. "I'll take you on a sleigh ride another day, little angel," he promised her.

Because they would be gone for hours, Brie excused herself and returned to the train car to nurse Anthony in comfort and warmth. She stared out the window at Sir and Rytsar while the baby nursed. Based on the serious expressions on their faces, the conversation they were having was tense.

Despite their obvious misgivings, Brie had remained

steadfast in her decision to see Lilly. It was important for her to see the girl in person. She needed to judge for herself what kind of threat Lilly still posed. Rytsar wanted her dead, believing there was no hope for rehabilitation, but Brie couldn't stomach the idea.

As Brie put Anthony down for his nap, she realized this trip was about her, not Lilly. This was about her own peace of mind.

The sleigh ride through the icy tundra ended up being incredible. If it hadn't been for the serious nature of the trip, she would have enjoyed the experience even more. Sadly, all she could think about was her impending encounter with Lilly, and she couldn't seem to concentrate on anything else.

That changed when they pulled up to the convent. Brie was struck by the simple beauty of the place. In the vast land of wintery emptiness, it was truly a beacon of hope.

Rytsar helped her out of the sleigh, and the three of them entered the holy place together. Several nuns greeted them, taking their coats, and handing them cups of warm tea after their cold journey.

Brie sighed with pleasure as she wrapped her freezing hands around the warm mug and took a sip. "Just what my soul needed," she murmured.

The eldest nun escorted them to see the Reverend Mother, stating, "She has been anxious to meet you."

The moment Brie entered her office, she was struck by the calm wisdom of the woman. Although her face was withered and old, her eyes shone with an inner light. When Rytsar introduced Brie, she immediately knelt, bowing low on the floor.

"Please, child. Do not bow to me. I'm not God."

Brie quickly got back on her feet, explaining, "I am indebted to you for keeping me and my daughter safe."

The Reverend Mother motioned her to approach. "Let me get a good look at you." As she looked Brie over, she muttered to herself, "I better understand why she wanted to extinguish your light."

Brie looked at her, confused.

Sitting back in her chair, the Reverend Mother told her, "I made a vow to God to help that wayward child." Shaking her head, she added sadly, "I have failed in my mission."

"No," Brie protested. "It is not your fault that Lilly refuses help."

The Reverend Mother raised her palm to silence Brie. "I was charged to bring the girl into the light, yet she remains cemented in darkness."

The revered woman glanced at Rytsar. "It is my biggest regret."

"Some cannot see the light," Rytsar replied coldly.

She shook her head. "I refused to believe that. The fault lies with me, not the girl."

"You are wrong, Reverend Mother," Rytsar insisted.

When the venerable woman narrowed her eyes, Rytsar immediately bowed his head. "But I respect your thoughts on the matter."

Sir spoke up. "I apologize for my sister's many offenses against you."

She turned to address him. "You have nothing to apologize for, Mr. Davis." Shifting in her chair, she added, "Thankfully that unwanted attention stopped recently."

"I am relieved to hear that," Sir replied.

Brie was grateful Lilly was no longer stalking the Reverend Mother with her sexual advances. She took it as a positive sign of growth.

The Reverend Mother glanced wearily at Rytsar before stating, "You will find the girl resting in her room. You should know, I did not inform her you were coming. It was not worth the chaos it would evoke."

"Thank you, Reverend Mother," Brie said, eternally grateful to the woman. If it hadn't been for her constant vigil over Lilly, there was no telling what havoc Lilly would have caused.

One of the nuns escorted the three of them to a lovely courtyard as they made their way to the other side of the nunnery. The chill of the freezing wind only added to the chill in Brie's bones as she drew closer to Lilly's room.

She noticed there were two nuns seated on either side of the door, silently reciting their prayers over their rosaries.

"I will remain outside. Call out if you need assistance," the nun who had escorted them said.

"Are you certain you want to do this?" Sir asked Brie, clearly concerned for her well-being.

Although she could barely breathe, she nodded. "I

am, Sir."

Sir opened the door and was the first to step inside. Brie knew he would protect her from Lilly should she make any move toward Brie.

When Brie entered the room, she was surprised to find the girl sleeping. She looked innocent and vulnerable in that state…it stirred something inside Brie.

Lilly was simply the product of a terrible mother and her own mental illness. For a moment, Brie actually felt compassion for the girl.

That all changed the moment Lilly opened her eyes and stared at Brie.

The moment their eyes met, Brie's heart skipped a beat. She felt she could see straight into Lilly's soul, and all she saw there was malevolent darkness.

Lilly broke the gaze, leaving Brie breathless. Sitting up slowly, she completely ignored Sir, turning all her attention on Rytsar.

"I knew you would come back for me," she said in a sweet voice, then pouted. "But why did you have to bring *her*?"

Rytsar snarled. "Not another word."

Sir stepped in front of Brie protectively. "We are not here to play childish games, Lilly."

Her expression grew ugly and she cried shrilly, "Get out, both of you!"

"Enough," Rytsar barked.

Lilly shivered in delight. "I love it when you get all domineering with me."

Brie stared at her in shock. Why the hell was Lilly flirting with Rytsar? He was the one who captured and tortured her until he was able to squeeze out the truth about her plans to harm Brie and the baby.

Suddenly recalling Faelan's warning the day before, Brie realized *this* was the "freaky shit" he had been talking about.

Sir took command of the situation. "We are only here for a short time. If you have anything to say to Brianna, say it now."

Lilly acted as if she hadn't heard him, continuing to completely ignore them both as she stared at Rytsar like a lovesick puppy.

When Brie tried to move toward her, Sir put his hand on her shoulder to stop her. Heeding his warning, Brie stayed where she was, but told Lilly, "I want to know one thing."

When Lilly didn't respond to Brie, Rytsar commanded, "Answer her truthfully."

Lilly let out a flirtatious laugh, batting her eyes at him before dutifully turning to face Brie.

The moment Brie tried to speak, fear closed her throat, making her momentarily mute.

"Well?" Lilly asked, a hint of a smile on her lips.

Even though she was terrified of Lilly's answer, Brie forced herself to ask, "Do you regret what you did to me or my daughter?"

Lilly stared at Brie for a long time before answering. "Yes."

Brie suddenly felt a surge of hope, and silently prayed Lilly would give her something to hold on to.

"The truth is, Brianna," Lilly said, her smile suddenly turning cruel, "I regret that you aren't living the life you were meant to."

"Meaning?" Sir growled ominously.

Lilly looked him dead in the eyes. "Don't play stupid with me, Thane. I think you know exactly what I mean."

Before Sir could respond, Rytsar kicked the door open and grabbed Sir and Brie, pushing them out of the room. The nuns rushed inside, subduing Lilly while Rytsar marched Sir and Brie through the hallways. The veins on Rytsar's neck pulsed with rage.

He kept his tight grip on Brie as he stormed through the courtyard, bypassing the Reverend Mother's office, as he marched straight to the sleigh. After helping Brie into it, Rytsar jumped in after Sir and barked, "Leave, now!"

The driver snapped the reins and the sleigh started off with a jolt. Brie sat there in stunned silence.

"I'm glad you pulled me out of there, brother," Sir confessed in a ragged voice. "I was about to end her life."

"I could tell, comrade." Sighing heavily, Rytsar made his own confession. "As you just witnessed, a new issue has arisen with the creature."

"Why didn't you tell us she switched her obsession from the Reverend Mother to you?" Sir demanded.

He shrugged. "There was nothing you could do, *moy droog*. I spoke with Dr. Volkov, and he informed me that the creature is suffering from a rare psychological condition called Stockholm syndrome."

Sir frowned. "I am familiar with the condition."

"It began with the Reverend Mother after she took over care of the creature but has since transferred to me."

Brie frowned. "Why?"

"He doesn't know, *radost moya*. But the good doctor has been consulting with top experts in the field to find answers."

"It's just so creepy." Brie shivered. "The fact she once claimed to be in love with Sir, but now acts like he doesn't exist because she's fixated on you? It doesn't make any sense!"

Rytsar crossed his arms. "Nothing the creature does makes sense."

Soul Check

On the trip back to Moscow, Brie's encounter with Lilly kept playing over and over in her mind. The girl had shown zero remorse for the monstrous things she'd done to Hope and Brie.

In Brie's heart, she knew Lilly would never change. While Brie hoped that Dr. Volkov could help her in some way, she didn't believe it would protect her from Lilly's wrath.

Looking at Rytsar holding her son in his arms, Brie knew beyond a shadow of a doubt that she would do anything to protect her children if Lilly ever tried to hurt them again.

"Would you have really killed her?" she asked Sir, who was reading a Russian newspaper beside her.

He didn't even hesitate as he closed the paper, "Yes."

Brie shivered, suddenly understanding the danger she had put them in because of her need to see Lilly. "I'm sorry."

He placed his hand on her thigh. "For what?"

"For making you go there. It was foolish of me to put you in that dangerous position."

"You didn't make me do anything," he corrected her. "I understood why you needed to see Lilly." He lifted her chin to look into her eyes. "Until you saw for yourself the threat she still poses to you and our children, you would have remained unsure. Now, any future decisions concerning Lilly will be easier for you to make."

"Do you think there's any possibility Dr. Volkov will be able to cure her, Sir?"

"No. However, I understand your need to try."

She glanced at Rytsar, telling Sir, "I can't believe he put himself through this for me, especially knowing how demented Lilly is now."

"Like me, he understands your need for this trip. I liken it to the situation I faced with my mother when she was dying. Until I was ready to let her go, I needed to keep her on life support."

Brie looked at him with sympathy.

"Had I pulled the plug too soon, I would have always questioned whether I made the right decision." He smiled sadly at her. "But, because I waited, I have never questioned it."

"What are you two talking about, looking all serious and glum over there?" Rytsar asked, holding Anthony up and smiling at him.

"I was just telling Sir how grateful I am that you arranged this trip. But I feel terrible knowing that I put you both in a dangerous situation."

"It was uncomfortable, yes. But never dangerous, *radost moya*. I had everything under control."

Brie shivered when she thought about Lilly's strange obsession with Rytsar. It was beyond disturbing…

"Do you think Lilly is suffering from Stockholm syndrome or just faking it?"

"I will let the doctor decide. Either way, it matters little to me."

Sir groaned. "I'm sorry my sister is putting you through this."

"*Half*-sister," Rytsar corrected him. He laughed it off. "Although her behavior is irritating, it's unimportant— like a gnat. Don't give it another thought."

Brie got up and walked to Rytsar, giving him a hug while he held the baby. "I don't know how I can ever repay you for everything you've done."

"Live a long and happy life, *radost moya*. That is all I ask."

Hope came toddling over, hugging Rytsar and Brie's legs as she looked up at them.

"Just when I thought *moye solntse* couldn't get any cuter…" he said, leaning down to scoop her up in his arm while still holding Anthony.

There was no better dyadya *in the world*, Brie thought, gazing at him lovingly as he cuddled her two children.

Rytsar surprised them both when he had them exit the train before their last stop. "There's something I want to show you."

Brie looked at Sir, who shrugged. It appeared he was equally clueless as they got in the vehicle that was waiting for them.

"I have been anxious to show you, *radost moya*. It has been many years in the making."

Rytsar glanced at Sir, grinning from ear to ear. "You won't believe it!"

His excitement was contagious, and he smacked the back of the driver's seat as he encouraged him to drive faster.

They eventually pulled up to a majestic building made of marble with the words "Tatianna Linguistic Preservation Center of Russia" carved into the stone at the top.

"Oh, Rytsar," Brie gasped as she got out of the vehicle. "The building is absolutely beautiful!"

He slapped Sir on the back as they walked to the entrance. "Do you remember when I started this project, *moy droog*?"

Sir smiled. "I do. Wasn't that almost fifteen years ago?"

"*Da!*"

Sir scanned the parking lot. "Although the building remains just as impressive, I don't remember the parking lot being jam-packed with cars."

"That's because the last time you visited, we had only a handful of languages preserved." He looked at the building proudly. "Now, we have over a hundred Russian dialects represented in the museum, as well as an extensive library for linguists. People from all over the world come here to learn and study the different dialects."

Brie's jaw dropped as she stared up at the massive building. "I had no idea, Rytsar!"

"This is nothing. Wait until you see what's inside!" Lifting Hope onto his shoulders, he headed to the entrance.

Tears pricked Brie's eyes when they stepped inside and she saw a giant mural of Tatianna. Under the image was a quote from her. "Before we lose our older generation, I want to record their stories in their native languages and interpret them for future generations."

The girl looked so young and beautiful…

Rytsar pointed to the hundreds of artful displays that filled the large floor space. "Each display includes photos of the people, along with recordings of their native tongue and information about their culture." He then pointed to the left. "On this side is the library…" then pointed to the right. "…and on this side, we have a collection of classrooms, meeting rooms, and private research areas."

Sir shook his head in admiration. "You never cease to amaze me, Durov. Tatianna would have been proud of this institution."

"She is," he answered confidently.

"What an incredible homage to her, Rytsar," Brie choked out, moved beyond words. "A living testament to her beautiful vision."

"Only the best will do," he replied, clearly pleased by her reaction.

One of the staff members helping on the floor recognized Rytsar and began clapping. Soon, the entire room echoed with applause for him.

Rytsar placed his hand over his heart and pointed to Tatianna's mural before turning away and heading to the entrance doors.

Brie followed behind with Sir. She took one last look at Tatianna's beautiful face smiling at her on the wall. "Your spirit lives on, Tatianna."

That night, Brie left the warmth of the bed to nurse Anthony. Although the apartment was dark and silent as the grave, she didn't mind. Brie enjoyed looking at the city lights of Moskva-City from eighty-five stories above it.

It was so peaceful from way up here.

The hairs on Brie's neck stood on end when she heard someone cry out behind her. Clutching Anthony against her chest, she turned and scanned the darkness, whispering, "Is anybody there?"

After several moments, she added a warning, "Rytsar, you better not be trying to scare me."

Brie did not hear another sound. She knew this place was heavily guarded, so there was no chance an intruder had managed to sneak in. After several more minutes, Brie started to wonder if she had imagined it and relaxed.

She settled back on the couch and continued to nurse her son.

"Brie…"

She whipped around to see a shadowy figure standing there. Before she could scream, he covered her mouth.

"It's just me, blossom."

Brie slowly relaxed, but the moment he pulled his hand away from her mouth, she hissed at Faelan, "Why did you sneak up on me like that?"

"I'm sorry," he whispered. "I just woke up from a dream and needed to talk to someone."

Taking a deep breath trying to calm herself, Brie set Anthony down and adjusted her clothing before scooting over to make room for Faelan on the couch.

While she waited for him to speak, she gently rubbed Anthony's back. Because her eyes had adjusted to the dark, she could see the expression on Faelan's face. It was almost…radiant.

"I had a dream about her," Faelan began.

"I trust it was a good one."

She could hear the smile in his voice when he answered, "It was."

Brie turned to face him, wanting to give him her undivided attention. "I would love to hear about it."

He sighed, but the sound of it was light, not heavy. "It was as if Kylie never left. We were walking on the sandy beach. I could feel the warmth of her hand in mine as a cool breeze played with her hair."

"What happened in the dream?"

"She kissed me…" He suddenly became silent, as if he were reliving the kiss. "I caressed her cheek and told her that I would never love another." His voice broke when he asked, "Do you know what she said?"

"What?" she gently urged.

He paused for a moment, closing his eyes as he repeated Kylie's words, "You were meant to love passionately. I want you to love another.'"

Faelan broke down, sobbing quietly. "It broke my heart."

Feeling the immensity of his pain, Brie moved closer, wrapping her arms around him. Rather than saying anything, she allowed Faelan to release all the pent-up anger and grief he'd suffered after Kylie died.

Brie held him tight until he finally chose to break the embrace. Swiping his eyes with his forearm, he confessed, "I think she was talking about our daughter. All this time, I've seen the baby as a constant reminder of what I lost." Another sob escaped him when he admitted, "I was wrong..."

Brie held her breath.

He looked up, staring at her through the darkness. "That little girl is my closest connection to Kylie."

"Yes!" Brie whispered.

"I wanted to give her up, Brie—but I can't."

"And Kylie wouldn't want you to."

"But her parents know how to raise a child. What if I fuck up?"

"Her mom and dad didn't know any more than you do when they had Kylie. The only thing Grace needs is to be raised with love."

He shook his head, looking at her doubtfully. "You really think it's that simple?"

"I know it is."

Faelan let out a ragged sigh. "I can't leave until Lilly

is transferred and securely locked up."

"I'm sure Rytsar can handle it on his own."

"I'm not staying for him. This is for *my* sanity. I can't rest until I know she is no longer a threat—to your family or my little girl."

"Maybe you can ask Marquis to stall them to give you more time."

He nodded. "It's worth a shot."

Brie grabbed Faelan's hand and squeezed it. "I know this is a big step, but you are not alone."

"I thought I heard voices," Rytsar muttered as he walked up. "Starting the party without me, are you?"

Brie looked up to see him dressed only in his underwear. It was an impressive sight.

"Get some pants on," Faelan complained jokingly.

"What? Can't handle the view?" Rytsar chuckled.

Faelan shook his head, moving over so Rytsar could sit next to Brie.

"Is everything all right?" Rytsar asked as he settled down on the couch and picked up Anthony, laying him against his chest.

Faelan nodded.

"Excellent."

He then turned to Brie. "And you, *radost moya?*"

"Other than Faelan scaring the bejeebers out of me, I couldn't be better."

Anthony made a cute little sound as he slept.

"They're so small and fragile," Faelan commented.

"You'd be surprised. They're hardier than you think," Rytsar stated, placing Anthony on Faelan's lap without asking.

"What are you doing, man?" Faelan protested.

"Relax and let it happen," Rytsar commanded in the same tone he used with his subs.

Faelan froze when Anthony started wiggling in his sleep. He let out a tiny burp before settling back to sleep.

"You'll find them quite calming when you give them a chance," Rytsar assured him. "In fact, I like them so much, I've asked *radost moya* for three more."

Brie giggled.

Faelan stared down at the sleeping child. "Do you really think I can do this?"

"*Da*," Rytsar answered with authority. "Keep your eyes on the horizon and never stop moving toward it. I believe in you."

To Nonna with Love

Brie glanced out of the window and looked down at the snowy landscape of Rytsar's beloved motherland. She hated to leave Russia, even though she was excited about where they were headed. There was nothing as good for the soul as a visit with Sir's grandparents, Nonno and Nonna.

Rytsar had insisted they ride to Italy in his jet, and he refused to take no for an answer, telling them, "I have hired the best pilot money can buy to fly me around the world. I trust no one else to get you there safely."

Brie was grateful for his thoughtfulness. Although she felt brave enough to go on the commercial flight Sir had booked, nothing could beat the comfort and service she would experience on Rytsar's private jet.

When it came time to take off, Sir double-checked to make sure the children were buckled in, then he sat down beside Brie and took her hand. "The first time is always the hardest."

She didn't think it would be an issue for her until the

jet was taxiing down the runway and the pilot announced they were cleared for takeoff. Out of nowhere, her heart started to race and her body tingled from the crown of her head all the way down to her fingers. Brie found it hard to breathe as an acute sense of doom consumed her.

"Sir…"

"Everything is fine," he said calmly. "Take in deep breaths, and let them out slowly as you count backward from a hundred."

Brie obeyed without question, even though she felt like they were about to die. Closing her eyes, Brie concentrated on her breathing as she counted, "One hundred, ninety-nine…"

As the jet sped up, she dug her fingers into Sir, her nails clawing his thigh.

Brie let out a frightened cry when she felt the plane lift off.

"Keep counting, babygirl," he commanded gently.

Brie lost count and had to start back at a hundred, her whole body shaking when the jet made a sharp right.

"Count out loud."

Brie forced herself to speak but had to concentrate hard to say each number aloud. Once the plane began to level off, he reached over and gave her a hug. "You did well."

Tears filled her eyes when she asked, "Do you go through that every time you fly?"

He looked at her with sympathy. "Like I said, the first time is the hardest. It will improve with time, babygirl."

Still shaking like a leaf, she confessed, "I don't know if I will ever fly again after this trip."

He chuckled lightly. "I felt the same, but as I said before, the alternative takes up a lot of precious time. And even then, every mode of travel contains risks."

Feeling immense sympathy, Brie looked at Sir. "I never understood how much you suffered."

He waved off her concern. "I make my choices and am willing to live with the discomfort because I am a practical man."

Brie leaned her head against his shoulder. "I humbly disagree, Sir. What you are is a courageous man."

He smiled, kissing her on the cheek. "Leave it to my sub to stroke my ego."

"I'd be happy to stroke something else, Sir."

His light laughter delighted her. Then he leaned in and told her, "I will be taking you up on that later tonight, téa."

I'm melting…

Being on a private jet, they were able to fly direct, which made it only a four-hour flight to Isola d'Elba.

Brie had to admit that Sir was right about the convenience of airplane travel. As the jet readied to land, instead of counting, she imagined what he would be doing to her that night in every explicit and delicious detail…

Brie was as charmed now by Portoferraio as she'd been

the first time Sir took her to visit his father's hometown. The ocean view from the Italian city was breathtaking, but it was the town itself and the gregarious people she found absolutely enchanting.

She couldn't hide her smile as they walked the narrow streets of old apartments, with their colorful doors and shutters.

Sir placed one hand on her back while he carried Hope. Two women walking by recognized him and waved.

Hope's face lit up, and she waved back. Soon she was waving at every person they saw. The townspeople responded to her, waving back at Hope with the same enthusiasm. Their little girl totally ate up the attention.

It warmed Brie's heart that the Italians genuinely adored children. Here in the old country, they were loved and appreciated for their energy and innocence. It was refreshing. In Los Angeles, Brie found that strangers tended to treat her children like unwanted distractions.

As the two of them started up the steep hill to his grandparents' place, Brie felt her excitement grow. Sir's family was like a giant blanket of love.

Their family bonds were tight, but they had enough room to enfold Brie in it. The first time Sir introduced her, she hadn't known any Italian, and yet they still made her feel a part of the family.

Under Sir's careful instruction, she had come to learn enough Italian to understand and interact with them. His family had shown a deep appreciation for her willingness to learn their language, which made the familial bonds even stronger.

Walking up the steep flight of steps that led to the apartments, Brie admired the magenta bougainvillea that graced the walls and fences of many of the buildings. Not only were they beautiful but, for Brie, they held a sentimental value. They had been part of her wedding bouquet and were also used as a decoration on the cake.

The truth was, everything about Portoferraio enchanted her!

Sir had chosen not to inform his family they were arriving five hours earlier than expected, so his grandparents thought they were due in the late afternoon based on their original flight.

"I don't want my grandmother to wear herself out rushing around, trying to make things perfect when all we want is to spend time with them," he explained.

When they finally made it to the top, Brie was surprised to see the bright red door was covered in huge blue ribbon with Anthony's name embroidered on it in beautiful script.

"I see Aunt Fortuna has been busy," Sir said, smiling as he knocked on the door and waited.

Similar to their past visits, Nonno and Nonna's neighbors peeked out their windows, whispering excitedly to each other when they spotted the famous violist's son, Thane Davis. Especially now that he had come all the way from America with the new baby.

Hope waved to them all, giggling in delight when they waved back and cooed at her.

Brie could hear Aunt Fortuna's voice as she walked down the stairs. She was complaining bitterly in Italian as she approached the door. "Who is bothering us at this hour when they *know* the Davises are coming…"

The moment she swung the door open, her jaw dropped. Quickly stepping outside, she shut the door behind her. "You're not supposed to be here yet! We still have five hours."

"Surprise!" Brie shouted, giggling.

Aunt Fortuna grinned at Hope as she complained sweetly, "How can it be you're growing up so fast, sweet child?"

She then looked at Anthony and let out a little cry of joy. When Sir tried to hand him to her, she backed away. "I can't. My sister must be the first one to hold him. But…" She took a step closer and sighed. "Look what a handsome boy he is!"

Aunt Fortuna smiled as she glanced up at Sir. "Rosanna is going to be so happy to see him."

She then looked at Brie lovingly. "All of you."

Then her expression suddenly changed, and she started pushing Thane away from the door. "But not yet. Not until we have the place ready for your visit."

Sir stood his ground. "I'm not leaving. I came to see Nonno and Nonna." He swirled his hand in the air dismissively. "Not whatever else you may have planned."

"You don't understand! We're still preparing the meal, and there are tables to be set, and then the home to be tidied…"

Sir scoffed, "Do you think I care?"

"It would be an honor for me to help with the cooking and cleaning," Brie told her.

"You are the special guests!" she cried.

Chuckling, Sir chided his aunt, "We want to be treated like part of the family, Aunt Fortuna."

Her eyes softened, but then she warned him, "Your grandmother is not going to like this."

Sir glanced at the baby in his arms. "Do you honestly think she'll care once she holds the baby?"

Signing, Aunt Fortuna looked up at all of the neighbors who had been watching them with interest. "I suppose not…" Shaking her head, she opened the door and gestured for them to come inside.

As Brie started up the narrow flight of stairs, she heard a flurry of activity taking place above. When she reached the top, she was hit by the incredible smells already wafting from the kitchen, and saw an impossibly large number of people scurrying around the cramped apartment.

"Look who's here!" Aunt Fortuna announced.

Everyone turned and froze, staring at them in stunned silence.

"You're early, *Nipotino*!" Nonna exclaimed.

A warm smile spread across Sir's face as he walked over to his grandmother. "I couldn't wait for you to meet our son."

The room echoed with "awws" as Sir placed Anthony in the tiny woman's arms.

She stared down at him, a look of wonder on her lovely face. "He is beautiful…"

Looking up at Brie, she asked with gentle concern, "How are you feeling, Brianna?"

"Wonderful," she answered, tears of happiness filling her eyes. "Especially now that we can be here with you."

Nonna held out a withered hand and grasped Brie,

pulling her close. "You cannot know the joy this brings me." Looking up at Nonno, she smiled. "To both of us."

Nonna handed Anthony over to her husband, saying with a catch in her voice, "Doesn't he look just like Alonzo?"

Nonno gazed intently at the child. "Yes. I would not know the two apart…" Cradling the baby in his arms, Nonno announced proudly, "Here is our newest member of the family, Anthony Alonzo Davis."

The entire room broke out in cheers, and then everyone gathered around the small child, each wanting to personally welcome him into the family.

Hope was not left out. Aunt Fortuna took her from Brie's arms, telling Hope, "Your favorite aunt has a special batch of my risotto for you. But I haven't cooked it yet because your papa came too early. Come to the kitchen and I will teach you my secrets."

Brie looked at Sir, her heart bursting with joy. "I love your family!"

He put his arm around her, smiling at them all. "They're not too bad."

Famiglia Ties

B rie spent the afternoon rushing from the kitchen, up to the rooftop, and then down again, doing whatever she could to prepare for the big celebration dinner. Being a part of it, seeing the way the food was made, and the interactions between the family members, was a whole new experience.

All she had ever gotten to see before were the end results of their labor. But this…this was the stuff life was made of! The bad jokes, their ribbing each other, the sibling rivalry, the taste-testing as they went, even the bumping into each other in the cramped space…all of it was a part of who they were as a family. When the family members got together, they became a unit on a mission, and Brie loved every minute of it.

Partway through the amiable chaos, she had to stop and take a moment to feed Anthony. She welcomed the break because it gave her a chance to sit with Nonna out on the balcony while she nursed.

"Come sit with me, *Nipotina!*" Nonna insisted. "You

shouldn't be running around so much," she scolded. "As a new mother, you shouldn't push yourself so hard."

Brie grinned, touched by her concern. "Don't worry, Nonna. Your grandson always makes sure I get plenty of rest."

*Among other things…*she silently added.

Nonna looked at Brie, her eyes shining with love. "You are a good mother, Brianna."

The compliment meant so much coming from Nonna. Brie glanced down at Anthony and confessed, "I love being a mom. It's the most rewarding thing I've ever done." Leaning closer, she whispered, "Even better than the films I create—but don't tell anyone!"

Nonna's eyes sparkled with interest. "Thane mentioned you had a big project coming up next summer. What is this film about?"

In her excitement, Brie had completely forgotten Sir's grandparents had no idea what kind of films she made. Thinking fast on her feet, Brie told her, "It's a documentary about different couples and how they express their feelings for each other."

Nonna glanced at her husband, who was busy directing everyone, and smiled. "What a wonderful project. Love looks different for every couple." Turning back to Brie, Nonna added, "When you find the right partner, it changes everything."

"I couldn't agree more, and I'm really proud of this film…" Wanting to change the subject before Nonna asked any more questions about it, Brie looked down at Anthony and cooed, "…but not nearly as proud as I am of this adorable bundle of cuteness!"

When she looked up, she noticed a sadness in Nonna's eyes she hadn't expected to see, and asked, "Are you okay?"

The kind old woman smiled, trying to cover up her sorrow. "I can't believe how much your son looks like Alonzo." She stared at him, and said in a wistful voice, "It's almost like going back in time every time I look at him."

After several moments lost in her thoughts, Nonna shook her head, laughing softly with tears in her eyes. "Don't mind me, *Nipotina*. I'm just a foolish old woman."

Brie reached out to grasp her hand. "No, you're not! You are the lifeblood of this entire family. *Nothing* about you is foolish, Nonna."

Her tears left Brie wondering if having Anthony here actually hurt Nonna because he reminded her too much of her son who committed suicide. Such a profound loss would never stop hurting, no matter how many years passed.

Nonno joined them on the balcony once Brie had finished nursing. "My beautiful granddaughter, you have made this old man happier than you know," he told Brie, his voice full of pride.

He glanced at his wife, and she nodded in agreement.

Sir's grandfather looked back at Brie with intense love. "To have a strong boy to carry on the Davis name is a priceless gift."

Nonna suddenly broke down. Quickly excusing herself, she hurried off to their bedroom.

Sir immediately walked over and asked, "What just

happened?"

His grandfather cleared his throat before answering. "It's a momentous, but emotional, day for my sweet Rosanna."

Aunt Fortuna popped into the conversation, adding her two cents. "I warned you that my sister would be upset. She wanted everything to be perfect."

Brie gave Sir a worried look.

She knew that Nonna's reaction had nothing to do with them arriving early. Brie sensed there was something much deeper going on. Something Nonna was keeping closely guarded even though it was obvious it was causing her unbearable pain.

But, surprisingly, by the time the meal was ready to be served, Nonna had rejoined the family and returned to her usual jovial self. "Let's eat!" she cried out, shooing everyone up the stairs to the rooftop.

As guests of honor, Sir, Brie, and the children were seated to the right of Nonno. Rather than sit in her normal place on his left, Nonna held Anthony and insisted on sitting next to Hope. The contentment on her face helped ease Brie's troubled heart.

With a proud smile, Nonno stood up at the head of the table. Raising his glass of wine to the heavens, he thanked God for a healthy child, then looked at Anthony resting in Nonna's arms and added, *"Cento di questi giorni!"*

Everyone raised their glasses, repeating the phrase before taking a drink.

Brie knew the words literally meant "wishing you a hundred days like this one" but the true sentiment behind it was to wish their son a long and healthy life. It was a traditional toast that took on a much deeper meaning for the family.

It was sobering to think that Anthony would be the only one to carry on the Davis surname, despite the huge family sitting around at the table. However, Brie also knew the love represented at this table was true and enduring. Whether by blood or marriage, they were all *famiglia* because of their beloved matriarch. Nonna had nurtured the strong bonds that defined this family, and Brie hoped she understood how treasured she was.

Looking down the long table, Brie was impressed that every inch of it was claimed by large dishes of food made with love and fresh ingredients. Brie challenged herself to take a small portion of everything that was offered, not wanting to miss out on an ounce of that love.

Sir looked at her full plate and winked at her. He obviously found it amusing, probably recalling the first time she had come to Italy. Back then, she had been extremely cautious about eating the food. But, being from America, how could she know how incredible it was?

Aunt Fortuna misunderstood her desire to try a little of everything and told her, "A new mother needs extra food to nourish the baby. You have not taken enough!"

Brie's eyes widened as each woman got up from the table and came to her with the particular dish she had prepared, putting an extra helping of it on Brie's plate. There was no possible way she could eat everything on the plate, but she also was desperate not to offend anyone.

With all eyes on her while she ate, Brie made certain to take several forkfuls of every dish, smiling after tasting each bite—everything from the cheesy polenta and tender gnocchi to the ribollita soup, salt-roasted shrimp scampi, and Aunt Fortuna's beloved risotto. After Brie had savored a taste of every portion on her plate, she began to slow down. Thankfully, Sir took pity on her.

Placing his finger under her chin, he leaned in for a kiss. The women at the table breathed out a collective sigh. After giving her a long and tender kiss, Sir pulled away and shrugged, smiling apologetically to his family. "My beautiful wife seems to have suddenly lost her appetite."

"I wonder why?" his cousin Benito teased. "Are you determined to make another *bambino* at the table, Thane Davis?"

The other men chuckled good-naturedly.

Nonchalantly pushing the plate away from Brie, Sir turned to Hope and offered her a bite of risotto. Hope's enthusiasm for her dish thrilled Aunt Fortuna, and she insisted to everyone at the table that it was Hope's favorite. Her declaration started a humorous battle between the women about who was the best cook.

Brie sat back and watched in amusement, drinking in every minute of it. She glanced at Sir and mouthed the words *Thank you.*

He smiled, then leaned over and whispered, "I wanted you to save room for tonight."

Brie blushed, both shocked and pleased that he was flirting with her in front of his grandmother, seated right beside him.

Here they were married, with two children, and this sexy man was still seducing her.

Be still my heart.

A Simple Request

That night, following a long session of fellatio, Brie lay in Sir's arms, purring in satisfaction. "I love pleasing you, Sir."

He kissed her on the lips. "I crave the connection with you."

She lifted her head and looked up, smiling at him tenderly. "It's a rare man who insists on making his sub come every session."

"It is purely a selfish act on my part," he told her, leaving a trail of kisses across her chest. "Listening to your mews of pleasure while your pussy pulses around my finger is something I never tire of."

She laid her head down on his chest, grinning. "And this little sub is extremely grateful for that."

When he chuckled, her head bounced lightly on his chest. She was silent for a moment before broaching the subject that had been worrying her all day. "Do you have any idea what's going on with Nonna? It broke my heart to see her so upset today."

Sir grunted. "I feel the same. I spoke to my grandfather about it because I was afraid she might be losing her eyesight again, but he assured me her health is fine."

"Does he have any idea?"

"Nonno basically repeated what he'd said earlier about this being an emotional time for her."

"I hate seeing her in pain, Sir. I just want to make her feel better."

Sir hugged her harder, pressing her against his chest. "I'm concerned about her as well, and plan to gently pry it out of her when we visit them tomorrow."

Brie instantly felt better. Whatever Nonna was dealing with, there was no reason she needed to bear it alone.

When they arrived at his grandparent's apartment the next morning, Brie was surprised to see Aunt Fortuna walking up to the door, too. The woman's eyes lit up the instant she saw Hope.

"Una!" Hope cried, wiggling in Brie's arms to indicate she wanted to get down.

The old woman's smile grew a mile wide when Brie set Hope down and the little girl ran to her. "Did you miss your Aunt Fortuna?"

Hope laughed as she was swept into her great aunt's arms.

"What are you doing here?" Sir asked as they walked up to the door.

"I wanted to check in on my sister and see this sweet

angioletto," she answered, squeezing Hope.

"I've come to speak to her myself," Sir informed her.

"Good." She nodded with a knowing expression. "No one listens to Aunt Fortuna, but I *knew* you coming too early would upset her."

Brie smiled, suspecting it was Aunt Fortuna who had been thrown by their early arrival.

Sir must have come to the same conclusion because he made it a point to say, "Aunt Fortuna, I'm certain you are right, and I feel that I must apologize to you as well."

His aunt smiled. "Well, I'm sure you learned your lesson and it won't happen again." She stood on her tiptoes to pat his cheek. "You're a good boy."

It tickled Brie to see his aunt treat Sir as if he were a child. No one else would ever dare to treat him that way. The fact that he put up with it was utterly charming.

"I'll be happy to take the children into the kitchen while you speak with Rosanna," Aunt Fortuna offered. She opened the door and called up the stairs to announce she was bringing the Davis family up with her.

Nonno met them at the top of the stairs. Even though the man seemed to be only skin and bones, his vitality filled the place.

Brie smiled as she handed Anthony to him, saying to her son in a sweet voice, "We have to get as much great-grandpa time as we can while we're here. Don't we, Antony?"

Brie caught Nonna staring at her husband with a look of longing on her face as he held the baby. When Sir leaned down to hug his grandmother, she grabbed his cheeks, pulling his face close to hers. "My sweet boy."

"I love you, Nonna," he said tenderly, enfolding her small frame in his embrace.

"Oh, how I wish you lived closer, *Nipotino*," she lamented when he finally let go.

Sir smiled, glancing at Brie. "We would if we could."

"I know, I know…your work requires that you live in America," she laughed lightly. "Don't pay me any mind."

"We are grateful you came to visit," Nonno told them as he handed Anthony to his wife. "We know it was not easy to travel so soon after the birth."

Nonna gently rubbed Anthony's cheek. "We cherish this time with him."

"We certainly do," Nonno agreed.

Aunt Fortuna called from the kitchen, "Nonno, our little Hope wants to show you something she made!"

"Coming." He grinned as he made his way to the kitchen to see what his great-granddaughter had made.

Brie understood Aunt Fortuna was giving Sir the time he needed to talk with Nonna, but she was uncertain whether she should stay or head to the kitchen herself.

The moment Sir put his arm around her, Brie had her answer. Being a direct man, Sir asked simply, "Nonna, why were you crying yesterday?"

His grandmother seemed startled by his question and kept her eyes on the baby as she continued to stroke his soft cheek. "It is nothing, *Nipotino*."

"Nonna…" His voice was gentle but commanding.

She glanced up at him but was hesitant to meet his gaze. "Some things are meant to stay buried."

"What things?" he urged.

She closed her eyes, the pain in her face easy to read as she fought to hold back her tears. "I can't...even ask it."

Sir let go of Brie so that he could walk Nonna to the couch, helping her to sit down. "You can ask me anything," he assured her.

When she was still hesitant, Brie asked her softly, "Would you like me to leave?"

Nonna held out her free hand. Brie stepped toward her, and Nonna pulled her toward the couch. "Please stay."

Brie sat down beside her, squeezing her hand gently in support.

"*Nipotino*," Nonna asked in a frightened voice, "we've never spoken about it...but you were there when Alonzo died."

When Brie saw Sir wince, she held her breath. She knew how traumatic his father's suicide had been for him.

Sir cleared his throat. "I was," he finally answered with reservation.

With tears running down her face, Nonna looked up at him. "What was his death like?"

It was not a question Sir was prepared for. He shook his head violently several times as if trying to stop the visions that were undoubtedly flooding into his mind.

Sir abruptly stood up and walked away from her, heading out to the balcony.

"I'm sorry, *Nipotino*..." his grandmother cried.

Meanwhile, Brie was left gasping for breath. Nonna's

simple question was heartbreaking to Brie, especially now that she was a mother herself.

No one should have to ask that about their own child.

Brie stayed with Nonna, but her heart longed to join Sir out on the balcony. She knew he was fighting old demons and it was clear from his posture that he was struggling to face them.

"I didn't mean…" Nonna whimpered, looking down at the baby, her face bereft.

"You did nothing wrong," Brie assured her as she glanced at Sir outside on the balcony. He had a death grip on the railing, his body rigid and unmoving.

After several moments, Nonna called out to him again. "I'm sorry, *Nipotino.*"

Brie watched Sir straighten his back and take a deep breath before walking back inside. "Do not apologize, Nonna. I was unprepared for the question, but you deserve an answer. Can we discuss this another day?"

Nonna quickly handed the baby to Brie and stood up. Sir embraced her small frame as she buried her face against him. Her heartbroken sobs cut right through Brie.

Sir closed his eyes as he comforted his grandmother, the two of them sharing a profound grief only they could know the depths of.

Brie cradled Anthony against her chest, silently praying that she would never know that kind of pain.

Finally, Nonna's tears stopped and she looked up at him with red-rimmed eyes. "*Nipotino*, I have a small request."

He looked down at her warmly. "What is it, Nonna?"

"Could…would…" she asked tentatively.

"Go ahead. Ask it," he encouraged.

"Could we christen the baby now, before you leave?"

Sir shook his head in confusion. "Nonna, Durov is the godfather and he can't come right now. He has important work to do."

Her face crumbled. "Please…" she begged.

Brie had never known Nonna to beg for anything.

Sir glanced at Brie helplessly as he held the tiny woman in his arms, completely at a loss. Brie shrugged, not knowing what to do.

Brie had wanted Rytsar to attend the christening. She knew it would be important to him because he took being their children's godfather seriously.

Sir looked down at Nonna with a forlorn smile. "Can I have time to think about it?"

Her bottom lip quivered. "If you must."

"I need to discuss it with my wife, Nonna."

She nodded, hugging him tighter before letting go. She then turned and gave Brie a hug.

Brie stared at Sir in concern as she embraced his grandmother.

Sir had the look of someone suffering from shell-shock. In a stoic voice he commanded, "Brianna, let's go for a walk."

The moment she heard him use her given name, Brie understood just how unsettled he truly was.

"Of course," she replied, taking the hand he offered her. Sir's fingers were cold as ice.

"Would you like me to watch Anthony while you

walk?" Nonna offered.

Brie nodded, handing the baby back to her.

She left with Sir in silence. A silence he didn't break until they reached the pier. Looking out over the water, he sighed raggedly. "I did not handle myself well back there."

Brie vehemently disagreed. "You couldn't have known what she would ask."

"I should have been better prepared. Hell, it's been almost twenty-five years since he died." He shook his head. "Twenty-five years...I can't believe it's been that long. It seems like yesterday."

Brie wrapped her arms around him, wishing she could absorb his pain so she could carry some of the burden.

"Nonna didn't ask about the details. I could have handled that, rattling off the details without even thinking about it like I did for the psychiatrists when I was a kid."

He sighed again, looking at her with pain-filled eyes. "No...she asked me what his death was like. Although the change in wording is subtle, that is a *very* different question."

Brie nodded, tears in her eyes.

"I was not prepared to answer because to do so would require me to relive what happened."

Brie held onto him even tighter.

Sir frowned, looking perplexed. "And, a christening? Why would she want to rush it? I don't understand."

His eyes were dark and troubled when he told her, "I don't believe in God, but we had Hope christened solely for my grandparent's sake. However…" He growled ominously. "…I don't appreciate being pushed, and Nonna is being uncharacteristically insistent about it."

She agreed. "It's not like her to beg."

"No, it's not."

Brie was surprised to hear a low chuckle behind her.

"Well, now, this is an unexpected surprise…"

His Answer

Brie turned to see Gino Mancini standing behind them. She'd forgotten how strikingly handsome the man was with his salt-and-pepper hair and classic Italian good looks.

He smiled warmly at Sir, holding out his hand. "Here I am on my way to meeting with a client, and I suddenly run into you. How have you and your beautiful family been?"

It took a moment for Sir to gather himself enough to take Gino's hand and shake it. He glanced at Brie, the pain still in his eyes, but answered, "We are well."

Brie caught people staring at Gino and even whispering amongst themselves as they walked by. He was a very important man in Italy. She assumed he must have to deal with that kind of attention constantly—especially on an island as small as Isola d'Elba.

While it made the situation that much more uneasy for the two of them, Gino seemed completely comfortable with it. "What brings you from America?"

Brie spoke up, wanting to give Sir time to recover. "We came to visit the grandparents with our children."

He cocked his head, his smile growing wider. "Children?"

"Yes," Brie stated proudly. "We now have a son."

"That is wonderful news. Congratulations!"

Gino turned to Sir. "Alonzo would be proud. This is cause for celebration. Please, let me take you out to lunch after my meeting."

Sir shook his head, answering stiffly, "I'm sorry we can't, but my wife and I appreciate the offer."

Putting his hand over his heart, Gino confessed, "When I think of all the things Alonzo has missed, it hurts me."

Sir cleared his throat, struggling to keep his emotions in check. "Yes."

Seeing Sir's discomfort, Gino thoughtfully turned to Brie and asked, "How is your film coming, Brianna?"

"Things are going exceptionally well," she replied, grateful to take the focus off Sir. "In fact, my next film is set to be released next summer."

He looked at her quizzically. "How can this be? You never returned to finish your research."

Brie understood his confusion and explained, "It's a different documentary I've been working on, Signore Mancini."

"Ah." He seemed to look at her with new admiration. "It appears you have been exceedingly busy since we last met."

Brie chuckled. "It *has* been a whirlwind."

"Does this mean you are shelving the documentary

on Alonzo?"

"Oh, no," she assured him. "I still have every intention of making Alonzo's documentary. It's just been put on the backburner for now."

"That is a shame to hear, but my offer remains." He gave her a charming grin. "You have an open invitation to come to my home anytime you wish to continue your research."

He glanced at Sir. "It would be an honor to have both of you visit my home."

Brie was grateful Gino had extended the invitation to Sir as well. The last time she'd gone, Gino traveled on business shortly after she arrived, making Sir uncomfortable about her going there unattended again.

Sir was gracious to him, explaining, "I appreciate the invitation, although I have no idea when we will be returning to Italy again."

Gino nodded. "I understand, Signore Davis. Know the invitation still stands." He smiled at both of them. "I look forward to meeting Alonzo's grandson someday. It will truly be a momentous occasion for me."

Sir's eyes softened. "As his son, it means a lot that you keep my father close to your heart."

"I think of him every day," Gino stated.

He said it with such sincerity, Brie believed him.

It must have touched Sir as well, because he held out his hand to Gino. "I'm grateful for this chance meeting, Signore Mancini."

Gino returned his handshake, saying amiably, "As am I. *Buongiorno*, Signore Davis."

He nodded to Brie before he turned to leave.

As Brie watched Gino walk away, she noticed several men following behind him. She suddenly realized that, like Rytsar, he was surrounded by a set of elite bodyguards.

It highlighted how important the man really was.

"It was good to see him," Sir stated as they watched him head into town. "It helps knowing there are others out there who value the memories they have of my father."

Brie took his hand and squeezed it. "People all over the world listen to his music, Sir. Alonzo Davis is a part of many lives."

Sir smiled at her. "I will hold onto that, babygirl."

They returned to his grandparents' apartment. But, on arrival, Sir did not speak to anyone, preferring to sit out on the balcony alone, lost in his own thoughts.

Nonna respected his need for solitude, but Brie noticed her glancing in Sir's direction, a worried expression on her face throughout the day. If it weren't for Hope's joyful energy, the day would have been difficult to get through.

To help pass the time, Nonna brought out a collection of small figurines she'd had carved when she was younger and showed them to Hope. The little girl's eyes lit up the moment Nonna opened the box and started taking out the wooden animals one by one. The carvings were simple, but perfectly represented each creature's characteristics. It made them easy for Hope to identify.

She played with them for hours, insisting that her great-grandparents join her on the floor in her make-believe world. It was adorable watching Nonno, a man with a usually serious demeanor, get down on his hands and knees and make the neighs of a horse as he galloped the figurine across the floor.

That is the beauty of children, Brie thought to herself.

Their joy was contagious and their imagination limitless. Hope's only mission was to play. Seeing Sir's grandparents respond to her daughter's enthusiasm with loving attention warmed Brie's heart even though she continued to worry about Sir.

Aunt Fortuna had taken Anthony with her into the kitchen while she was preparing the meal. Brie decided to join her so Hope and her grandparents could continue their play uninterrupted.

"How is Thane doing?" Aunt Fortuna asked the moment Brie sat down at the kitchen table.

Brie was uncertain how to answer because she was unsure what Aunt Fortuna knew about the situation. So, instead of answering her, she responded by replying with another question. "I can't tell. He's keeping to himself. How is Nonna doing?"

Aunt Fortuna gave Brie a worried glance. "Roseanna refuses to talk about it. I have no idea what has her wound up so tight. I haven't seen my sister like this in a long time."

"At least she has you for support."

"I love Rosanna!" Aunt Fortuna stated fervently. She continued stirring the pot, lamenting, "There are times when the only way I can help her is by pouring my love into her food."

Brie smiled at Aunt Fortuna with new understanding. "Nonna is lucky to have you."

She stopped stirring for a moment and looked at Brie. "Rosanna has been my best friend all of my life, Brianna. That's why it hurts me when I see her in pain."

Brie looked at her with sympathy. "It must have been difficult when Alonzo died."

Aunt Fortuna shuddered, making the sign of a cross over her chest. "It is not something our family talks about." Concentrating her efforts on stirring the pot, she muttered, "Those were dark days."

Needing to lighten the mode, Brie asked, "Is there anything I can do to help?"

"Have you made malloreddus before?"

Brie sighed in disappointment. "I'm afraid not. I don't even know what it is."

"Good!" Aunt Fortuna exclaimed, sounding pleased. "I will teach you how to make it right."

She grabbed a large cutting board and placed it on the table next to Brie. She then picked up a round hunk of pasta dough resting on the counter, as well as a small wooden paddle. Taking a seat beside Brie, Aunt Fortuna divided the dough into four equal parts. She then took one of them and rolled it out, cutting it into long strips. Taking one of the strips, she rolled it into a rope and did the same with a second one. Setting them side by side, she quickly cut the ropes into a bunch of small nuggets.

Once she was done cutting them, she showed Brie the paddle and explained, "The grooves give the malloreddus their classic texture."

Aunt Fortuna took a piece of the dough and pressed it against the grooved paddle, rolling it forward with her thumb in a quick, fluid motion. Out popped a beautiful piece of pasta with pretty ridges. She did it slowly several more times so Brie could see it before going faster. It was amazing how quickly she could turn the pieces of dough into perfectly shaped pasta.

It was like magic!

"Now you try it," she told Brie.

Smiling confidently, Brie took the paddle from her and picked up a small piece of dough. Following Aunt Fortuna's instructions, she pressed it against the paddle with her thumb, but what she made was a sad, misshapen misfit—not like Aunt Fortuna's pasta at all. Blushing, she tried again, but with little better results.

Aunt Fortuna tsked. "It isn't difficult, Brianna. Even a young child can do it. Let me show you again."

Brie suddenly had flashbacks to her Training Center days and the dreaded omelet lesson. Leaning in for a closer look, Brie watched the woman work for several minutes before she attempted it again.

Much to her chagrin, the malloreddus still looked misshapen and sad. Brie's blush deepened as she stared at her pile of misfits.

Aunt Fortuna tsked again. Glancing at Anthony lying in the carrier, watching them both, she shook her head sadly and told him, "I bet you could do better."

Brie laughed. Determined to get it right, Brie spent time carefully shaping the little pieces of dough while Aunt Fortuna continued to cook. What would have taken Aunt Fortuna minutes to make took Brie an hour.

Even then, they weren't perfect, but Brie was pleased with her work because she'd poured a lot of love into each and every one of those little morsels.

"Those will do," Aunt Fortuna stated when Brie was finished, tossing the lot into a pot of boiling water. Coming from such an experienced cook, Brie took that as a compliment.

When Aunt Fortuna finally announced that dinner was ready, they all came to the table, including Sir. "Smells delicious," he complimented as they sat down to eat.

Encouraged by Sir's easy demeanor, Nonna asked hopefully, "Have you made a decision, *Nipotino?*"

"I have," he stated as he served himself, spooning a large portion of Brie's pasta onto his plate.

"Your wife made those," Aunt Fortuna interjected.

Sir looked at Brie, smiling. "You did?"

She nodded with pride.

Taking a forkful, Sir tasted it, a pleased look on his face. "This is delicious, babygirl."

Brie blushed. "The truth is, I only shaped the pasta. Aunt Fortuna did everything else."

Aunt Fortuna tsked. "You were supposed to take credit for it, foolish girl."

Brie giggled. "I can only hope to cook like you someday."

"If you move your family here, I will teach you everything I know," she promised, giving Hope a bite from her own plate. "Wouldn't you like that?"

Nonna's eyes never left Sir while she waited patiently for him to answer.

"As for your question, Nonna…" Sir stated, turning to face her.

Brie held her breath, afraid his answer might end up

hurting his grandmother, but he completely surprised Brie when he told Nonna, "Brianna and I have yet to decide. However, she has been given an opportunity to continue her research at Signore Mancini's. I plan to take him up on that offer and join her for the next few days. It will give us time to make a decision, and allow my wife to complete her research on Alonzo."

Nonna's eyes filled with tears. "Thank you, *Nipotino*."

"For what?" he chuckled. "I haven't given you an answer about the christening."

She reached out and patted his hand. "You are considering it. That's all I ask."

Looking at his grandmother tenderly, Sir told her, "I love you, Nonna."

"And I love you, *Nipotino*."

"No matter what our decision is, trust that we will do what we feel is best," he told her.

She looked at him gratefully. "I know."

Brie smiled to herself. She was in a state of pleasant shock. The day had started out so horribly, but she was ending it by eating a fabulous meal with the people she loved. On top of that, Sir had just given her the opportunity to delve into Gino's extensive collection again.

She was so happy, she wanted to pinch herself.

Whispers in the Dark

When Sir called Gino to accept his invitation to visit, Gino insisted on sending his driver to pick them up. Brie couldn't believe this was really happening.

"This was the last thing I expected," she admitted to Sir.

"I know this film is important to you, babygirl. It is to me as well." He softly brushed her cheek. "I remember that you said my father wrote letters mentioning Nonna. I'm hoping I can discover whatever is haunting her while you complete your research. I'm certain it will give us some needed clarity."

She looked at him in amazement. "That's brilliant, Sir."

He smirked. "I have my moments."

When Gino's driver came to pick them up, Brie gleefully kissed Hope goodbye. Then she hugged Nonna. "Thank you for watching her."

"It's my joy, *Nipotina.*"

Aunt Fortuna called out from the front window

above, "I will be spoiling her rotten while you are gone."

Brie laughed, waving up at her.

Before they left, Sir's grandfather asked to speak with them alone and waited until Nonna went back into the apartment with Hope.

His expression was serious. "Be gentle with Rosanna's heart. She has been through enough pain to last a thousand lifetimes."

Sir looked at him with compassion. "We have no desire to hurt her, Nonno."

He nodded curtly, then left them to rejoin his wife.

"I feel as if there is a chasm of secrets I know nothing about," Sir muttered as he took Anthony from her and they walked with the driver down the hill to the ferry.

Brie glanced back up at the apartment for a moment. She was curious about what her research would uncover.

She hoped whatever they discovered would not have the power to tear this beautiful family apart.

Hours later, when Gino's driver pulled up to his home, Sir let out a low whistle. Gino Mancini didn't own a home—it was an imposing mansion.

"I had no idea…all this time I thought Durov's family home was impressive," he said, chuckling lightly.

Several servants greeted them at the car and took their luggage and baby paraphernalia, while another escorted them to the entrance of the mansion. Brie looked up at the grand, nine-foot-tall doors. She felt a surge of excitement, remembering all the treasures that lay inside.

A line of servants stood on either side, bowing to them as they passed. Brie felt like royalty as they were escorted to the library and instructed to wait.

Gino's incredible library was etched in Brie's mind. The massive walls of the two-story room were lined with rare classics, including first editions of the greats like Charles Dickens, Leo Tolstoy, Mark Twain, and Mary Shelley.

"You have to see this!" Brie led Sir to the book encased in glass. "Gino has a partial copy of the Gutenberg Bible!"

"I've only heard about these but have never seen an actual copy." Sir leaned down to examine it more closely. "The penmanship is remarkably meticulous, but the artwork…" He shook his head in amazement. "It is truly awe-inspiring."

"I agree, Sir," Brie said excitedly. "I can't believe Gino owns it!" Glancing at the shelves, she asked him, "Who is your favorite author? I bet he has an original cop—"

The door suddenly opened, and Gino entered the room. The man was dressed in an exceedingly stylish black Italian suit. He looked as if he were about to attend an important event.

"I see you've made it safely," Gino stated, obviously pleased to see them.

"We have." Sir shook his hand. "Thank you for letting us come on such short notice."

Gino raised an eyebrow. "When I said you are welcome anytime, I meant it, Signore Davis." He then looked at the baby in Brie's arms. "Is this your son?"

Brie smiled as she walked up to Gino. "He is."

Gino looked down at their child with tears in his eyes. "I can't believe it."

"Would you like to hold him?"

He looked at them both. "Only if you'll allow it."

"Certainly," Sir chuckled. "As far as I'm concerned, you are part of the extended family."

Gino held out his arms to receive Anthony. When Brie gently placed him in his arms, it quickly became obvious he was unused to children by the stiff way he held the baby.

He looked at Anthony as if he were seeing a ghost. "How can this be?"

"What?" Sir asked.

Looking up, he said in astonishment, "It's as if I'm looking straight into Alonzo's eyes."

"Nonna did say he is the spitting image of Alonzo," Brie told him.

Gino glanced back at the child, his eyes flashing with pleasant surprise "It's a miracle!"

Brie blushed on hearing his elation for their son. "He is a miracle to us," she agreed.

The instant Anthony woke up and started to cry Gino awkwardly passed the baby back to Brie. She cradled him against her shoulder, rocking him gently, and Anthony instantly quieted.

Gino stared at the child in wonder, telling Sir, "Did I not say this would be a momentous occasion? Alonzo truly lives on in this child."

Sir nodded thoughtfully. "I'd like to think so."

"There is no reason to question it," Gino affirmed.

Smiling knowingly at Brie, he asked, "Would you like to get started on your research?"

Brie grinned. "How did you know?"

"It is written on your face, *bella donna.*"

Gino clapped his hands, ordering his servants to take them to the boxes. Brie walked through the halls of the mansion, reacquainting herself with the many rare pieces of art that graced this place.

"Look at that Sir!" she cried, stopping at a large glass bowl with vibrant colors and intricate designs. "It's Venetian. Do you remember our honeymoon?"

"I do," he murmured huskily, putting his arm around her.

Brie noticed the servants waiting patiently. She pecked Sir on the cheek and started following them again, anxious to get her hands on the letters. Her heart started beating faster as they approached the secluded room where she'd spent so many hours poring over Gino's wealth of materials. But this time would be even better because Sir was here.

She stepped into the room, breathing a sigh of contentment. To her delight, she found that Gino had equipped the room with a bassinet and a changing table with supplies.

Sir walked over to the large antique desk. "It appears they've already set up your laptop."

"Gino has thought of everything," Brie gushed when she spied the tray of teas and small sandwiches.

Sir smirked. "It seems Mancini may know you a little *too* well. You'll have no reason to leave this room."

"I know!" she agreed, pointing to the stack of wooden boxes decorated with music notes. "Now, I get to study them to my heart's content."

Sir stared hard at the carvings on the boxes. "I wonder if the mystery of the notes on the mask Dante made you are hidden somewhere in these boxes."

"Wouldn't that be wonderful?" Brie squealed. She felt like a kid on Christmas Day.

Sir put his hand on her shoulder. "I don't want you pushing yourself too hard. I know how you get."

"I promise, Sir," she vowed, looking at him gratefully. "With you here, I'll be able to get twice as much done."

He chuckled. "I like the enthusiasm."

"Now, let me find you that letter!"

Brie opened each box until she found the one she was looking for. "I put them all in chronological order, so they'd make better sense." Sifting through them, she spotted the one she was looking for and walked back to him.

"This is the letter I was talking about, Sir."

Sir sat down at the desk and slowly pulled Alonzo's letter from the envelope. After glancing at it briefly, he set it down and looked away.

"Are you okay?" she asked in concern.

Sir nodded, but wore a pained expression when he said, "His handwriting…" He paused for a moment, choking out the words, "…I didn't expect seeing his handwriting would hit me this hard."

"Would you like for me to read it to you?" Brie offered.

When he nodded, she picked up the letter. "Gino, God would not want me to abandon my mother right now. He would never require such a sacrifice! I'm not ignorant of the hit I will take professionally for backing out on this tour, nor the financial burden it will place on you, but I don't care.

"You called me selfish, but I vehemently disagree. I am a son first, and a violinist second. I would suffer hell before I forsake my mother. If this ends your support, so be it.

"I could not live with myself if I deserted my mother when she needs me most."

The words hung in the air after she finished.

Sir shook his head. "What could have possibly happened to Nonna that my father would forsake his livelihood to return home?"

Brie's eyes lit up when she remembered. "There was another letter he sent, but it was months after this one."

"Read it to me."

Brie returned to the box to find the letter. She glanced at Sir apprehensively before reading it. "Gino, my family is devastated. After so much loss, it seems unfair that my mother must suffer through it again. I need a few more months before I can consider your proposition. However, I'm interested in the charity event in Rome, and I am committing to that without hesitation.

"Despite your generous offer, I insist on paying you back for the financial debt you have incurred. The choice to cancel the tour was solely for personal reasons. Please take out a percentage of my future earnings until I have paid in full.

"Your friendship is important to me, and I refuse to let money get between us. Once I am certain my family no longer needs me, I will reach out to you concerning the American tour. Sincerely, Alonzo."

Sir shook his head. "He mentions so much loss and my grandmother suffering through it again. What loss is he talking about?"

"I have no idea, Sir, but I just noticed this." She pointed to the letter. "He said, 'my family' not 'my parents.' Do you think that means that Aunt Fortuna knows?"

"She must. My mother's bond with her is too strong for there to be any secrets between them."

"I wonder why they kept this a secret."

"I don't know, but it seems to me they want that secret to die with her." Sir sighed, then glanced at the boxes. "I trust there is something here that will shed some light."

If that was true, Brie fervently hoped they would not regret finding it.

Deeper Still

Brie and Sir spent hours poring over Alonzo's letters. Although Sir was intent on finding answers to Nonna's past, in his search he eventually came across the letters where Alonzo wrote about his love for Ruth. Brie knew Sir had finally reached his breaking point when he slammed down one of those letters on the desk and walked away.

Quickly placing Anthony in the bassinette, Brie walked over to him. "Are you okay, Sir?"

"How can I be? I'm reading my father's declarations of love to a woman who would eventually drive him to commit suicide."

"Those letters were difficult for me to read as well."

"If I didn't know how it ended, I would find his letters incredibly heartfelt and telling." Sir groaned angrily. "How could he have been so easily deceived by her?"

Brie was overcome with a sense of compassion. "I don't think he was, Sir. I believe they did love each other in the beginning. What I can't understand is why that changed."

Sir suddenly turned, his eyes flashing in anger. Taking her face in both hands, he demanded, "If you *ever* lose your love for me, tell me. Don't run around with another man."

Brie placed her hands over his and smiled up at him. "We are condors, Sir. I will always love you."

It took a moment for her words to sink in before she felt his body begin to relax.

Stroking her cheek with his thumb, Sir furrowed his brow. "I find myself at a loss, babygirl. Reading these letters…after finding out my grandmother is hiding something vital from me…it's beginning to feel as if my entire life is built on lies."

"No, Sir," she said gently, taking his hand and placing it over her heart. "My love is not a lie."

He nodded, kissing her on the forehead.

Glancing back at the letter, he told Brie, "It would be difficult for you to understand what I'm struggling with because you were born into a happy marriage. I have no such foundation to stand on. I don't believe I was born out of love but out of malicious deceit."

Brie remembered the video of Alonzo's first performance in America and went to the box to search for it. Holding up the tape, Brie asked Sir, "Did you read the letter when your father described his first performance in America?"

Sir nodded.

"I watched this video right after reading his letter and I noticed something at the end I think you should see when you feel ready."

"I am ready now."

She looked at him in concern. "Are you sure?"

"I am not a man to be controlled by emotions," he stated gruffly, sitting down on the couch. Brie placed the tape into the ancient VCR and turned on the television. Settling down beside him, she said, "You'll be grateful Gino preserved this moment. Your father's performance is truly inspired."

Sir put his arm around her. Taking a deep breath, he let it out slowly as if mentally preparing himself for battle.

When he nodded, she hit play and snuggled against him as the applause from the audiotape filled the room. She felt Sir stiffen when his father took the stage and the camera zoomed in on his face.

"Papa…" he whispered under his breath as Alonzo Davis looked into the camera and smiled as he placed the violin under his chin.

It began to sing as he slid the bow effortlessly over the strings, playing the first notes. Brie was as entranced now as she was the first time she'd watched his performance.

Alonzo's violin sang like an angel as he carried the entire audience on a journey through the power of his music. When Brie covertly glanced at Sir, she caught him staring at the screen with a longing she'd never seen before.

Quickly looking back at the television before he caught her staring at him, Brie was struck by how young and charismatic Alonzo was in the video. She could only imagine the feeling of loss Sir must be enduring as he watched.

He was right. As much as she wanted to, Brie could never understand what it felt like to question her past and the relationship between her parents. She'd been one of the lucky ones. Even though her father could be critical and overprotective at times, she never once doubted her parents' love for her—or each other.

Sir watched the entire performance, keeping his emotions in check. When the audience stood up to give him a well-deserved standing ovation at the end, Alonzo looked at the camera and winked.

Just like last time, Brie felt a thrill, as if his wink had been meant for her—but she knew better now. "Did you see that, Sir?"

He cleared his throat. "What?"

"His wink at the end."

Brie rewound the tape, explaining, "He's winking at someone, and based on when Alonzo starts mentioning Ruth in the letters, I believe he is winking at her."

Brie hit play again, pausing the tape at the moment he winked. "You do not have to question whether you were born out of love, Sir." Pointing at the screen, she told him, "This is the look of a man in love."

Later that evening, one of the servants knocked on the door to inform them that Gino had requested they join him in the dining room. Although Brie would have preferred to skip dinner altogether so she could continue her work, she reluctantly put down the letter she was reading.

After feeding Anthony and putting him down for a nap, she took Sir's arm and followed the servant through the long halls of the mansion.

Gino stood up when they entered the room. "Please sit. Dinner is about to be served."

One of the servants at the table pulled a chair out for Brie on Gino's right side, while Sir was directed to sit on the left. Brie stared at Sir from across the table while the servant placed a napkin on her lap.

"I felt this arrangement would allow the three of us to talk comfortably," Gino explained. "Tell me, Brianna, how is the research going?"

She smiled, genuinely excited to be here again. "I'm learning so much by reading more of his letters and being able to watch his performances on tape." Shaking her head, she confessed, "I can't believe Alonzo kept such a hectic schedule."

Gino chuckled. "Alonzo was an extremely motivated man. He was determined to get his music out to the masses, and no one could keep him from his passion."

Sir nodded. "My father was devoted to his violin."

Brie sat back as the servant placed a bowl of soup in front of her.

"You'll be glad to know I asked my chef to skip the first two courses, Brianna. I suspect you would rather return to your research than eat."

She blushed. "I appreciate that, Signore Mancini."

"Gino," he corrected her, raising an eyebrow. "I insist."

Brie looked to Sir, who nodded his approval.

She smiled at the kind man, "Thank you for your

thoughtfulness, Gino."

"My pleasure." He pointed to her soup. "I wanted to share a little about my family through this first dish. It was my father's favorite. Have you had minestra d'orzo before?"

She looked down at the warm broth, unfamiliar with the yellow color or the smell. "I don't think I have."

"It's a traditional barley soup."

Brie took a sip of the warm soup. It was a pleasant mixture of barley and smoked bacon, with a base of traditional vegetables and a sprinkling of chives. "Delicious," she told him, impressed by the taste.

Gino nodded, clearly pleased that she was enjoying it.

"Signore Davis," he said, turning his attention to Sir. "What is it like, going through your father's past?"

Sir pursed his lips and took a moment before answering. "It has been an emotional journey."

Taking a sip of the soup, Gino stated, "I can only imagine."

Sir suddenly put his spoon down. "I do have a question for you."

"Go on," Gino encouraged him while he continued to eat.

"In the letters, my father mentioned my grandmother was suffering. If I recall right, he specifically said she had suffered too many losses. Do you have any idea what he was talking about?"

"I discovered quickly that your family is extremely private. I could never pry what was going on with her out of Alonzo. Trust me, I tried—multiple times."

Sir frowned.

After taking several sips of the soup, Sir set down his spoon again. "Did you get a chance to see the mask Dante sent my wife?"

Gino smiled. "Yes. Truly a masterpiece fit for a queen."

"Did you happen to recognize the musical notes on it?"

Gino laughed. "I'm sorry—that detail escaped me."

"Do you mind if I get the mask and show it to you now? I feel certain I've heard the song before, but I can't place it."

"Certainly."

Brie perked up, surprised to hear that Sir had brought the mask with him. He returned with her mask a short time later and handed it to him before sitting back down.

Gino stared at the mask looking perplexed. He handed it back to Sir and apologized, "I'm sorry. It's only five notes."

"I realize that, but the combination is unique. I *know* I've heard it before."

Gino shrugged, picking up his spoon. "I wish I could help, Signore Davis. Fortunately for you, there will be a talented musician attending the gathering tomorrow. You can ask him then."

Sir glanced at Brie questioningly. She shook her head, as surprised to hear it as he was.

"What gathering?" Sir asked.

Gino sat back in his chair, addressing them both. "I hope you don't mind, but I have invited a few friends of Alonzo's to join us. It will give them an opportunity to see the child, as well as to reminisce about your father. I hope it will provide you with information you would not have otherwise."

"That is exceedingly kind of you. Thank you," Sir told him, clearly touched.

Late that night, after her eyes could no longer focus, Sir picked Anthony up from the bassinette and told Brie to follow him to bed. "It will still be there in the morning," he laughed when he caught her looking back at all of the boxes.

After setting Anthony in the antique crib in the guest room, Sir proceeded to undress her, then ordered her to bed.

After shedding his own clothes, he joined her. Brie cuddled against his naked body and confessed, "I'm suddenly not tired."

"Really?" he chuckled.

Brie was thrilled to be staying in the same room as before. It was impressive with its four-poster bed and red and gold bed curtains. "Did you know great artists throughout the centuries have slept in this very room?"

"They have, have they?"

Brie nodded. "Dante told me."

Sir asked with a playful smile, "What do you think they did on this bed, babygirl?"

"Sleep?" she giggled.

"I'm certain they did much more than that…why

else would it be so big?" Sir sat up and began untying the curtains. "I wouldn't want to scar our son with the wicked things I'm about to do to his mother."

Brie's eyes grew wide as he let the luxurious curtains close them in. "This feels so romantic."

"Tonight, you address me as Master."

Brie shivered in delight, excited by his command. "How can I please you, Master?"

He looked her body over hungrily and growled, "By letting me fuck that sweet little ass."

Brie cried out in surprise when Sir suddenly threw back the covers and flipped her over, grabbing her waist as he hoisted her up.

"Shh…" he warned her, slapping her on the ass. "We don't want to wake the baby or our host."

Brie squeaked, imagining Gino in the room across the hall. She covered her mouth, muffling her giggles.

"Such a bad girl…" he murmured, biting her fleshy ass before spanking it again. Sliding his hand between her legs, he began stroking her clit. "Do you think I can make this bad girl come?"

In her excitement, she momentarily forgot to call him by the proper name, and whispered, "Yes, Sir."

He slapped her ass harder this time. "What did you say?"

Brie loved the sting of his hand but dutifully answered, "Yes, Master."

He leaned in close, commanding, "Not another sound."

Brie nodded to indicate she understood. She was enjoying his forceful play, maybe a little too much. Oh,

God, she was wet…

Sir ran his hands over her body, telling her how rough he would be. In response, she lifted her ass higher, silently begging him to show her.

Sir pressed his fingers into her pussy, coating them with her juices, then rubbed them over his cock. He pressed his fingers into her again, telling her, "You are going to provide your own lubricant tonight."

Brie couldn't say why but the idea of that totally turned her on and she ground her pussy against his hand. After his cock was thoroughly coated with her abundant excitement, he positioned himself behind her.

"Bad girl…" he growled.

Brie stifled her moan when the head of his cock pressed against her tight hole, demanding entrance. This was her favorite part of anal sex, feeling her body physically surrender to his sexual desire.

"That's it…" he murmured as his cock breached her opening and slipped inside. Grasping her waist tighter, Sir grunted as he forced his shaft deep inside her ass.

It took everything in her not to cry out as she took the fullness of his shaft. He held her still for a moment, giving her time to appreciate just how deep he was before he began thrusting inside her.

Brie threw her head back, giving in to his lust as he stroked her ass mercilessly with his cock. In that moment, all the questions surrounding Nonna's past, all of the sadness and uncertainty caused by Alonzo's death, disappeared as they became one, giving in to their unbridled passion for each other.

It was glorious!

Unexpected Blessing

When Brie woke up the next morning, she parted the curtains to find Anthony quietly staring at her from the crib.

"My handsome little boy," she whispered as she leaned down to pick him up. Cradling his tiny body against her chest, Brie moved to a large chair and tucked her feet under her as she settled into it.

While Anthony nursed, Brie looked around at the art on the walls, all of it representing centuries of work. There was something sacred about connecting with the past, and Brie felt that had been lost in the fast-paced world of today. She was always moving forward, ready to conquer the next challenge, yet never took time to reflect on the past or the people who had gone before her.

She liked that about this house—about the Mancini family's mission to support exceptionally talented artists through countless generations. It preserved something vital that might benefit future generations if they took the time to reflect and learn from it.

Sir pushed the bed curtain away and stood up. Brie never ceased to be captivated by his naked body. The man was pure perfection.

"How are you feeling this morning, Sir?"

"Last night's romp definitely helped me release some pent-up tension."

She blushed. "I know I certainly enjoyed it."

As Sir slipped on his clothes, he asked, "What are your plans today? I want to be efficient while I work beside you so we can get the information we need and get back to my grandparents."

"Agreed, Sir. I plan to watch the rest of the videos and take down notes. That still leaves the remaining letters, the box of photos, another box with awards and news clippings, and finally the one with all of his record albums and sundry things."

He nodded. "I'll check through as many boxes as I can and document what I find."

"Perfect." Brie sighed, worried about the evening. "I hope this gathering tonight doesn't take too much of our time. There's still so much for us to go through."

"I feel the same, babygirl, but we have to look at it as another resource."

"You're right. I *am* grateful for the opportunity to speak to people who knew him outside the family."

"I agree."

Brie suddenly felt a check in her spirit. Looking at him with sympathy, she confessed, "I know I treat all this like a research project when it is extremely personal to you."

He smiled. "I actually prefer it, babygirl. It helps me

to process everything when I can take my personal emotions out of the equation."

She grabbed his hand. "If I ever say anything that offends you, please let me know. It's the last thing I want to do."

He gazed into her eyes. "I know your heart."

She hugged him, grateful that he knew her so well.

When they arrived at the study, Brie spied the breakfast tray. "I like that Gino understands there's no time to waste."

"As do I," Sir said, heading to the boxes. He opened each box, choosing to begin with the albums and musical sheets. Brie suspected he was on a mission to find the song that used those five notes since all of his searches on the internet had yielded nothing.

As for Brie, she enjoyed watching Alonzo grow as a musician in the videos. Although he was confident in his talent from the beginning, she could see that over time, he'd learned to connect with his fans on a personal level while on the stage. Another benefit of watching them was that the sound of his violin filled the room as they worked, bringing with it the passion and love that infused all of Alonzo's music.

Brie glanced at her son Anthony, grateful that he would grow up immersed in his grandfather's music. She then looked at Sir and noticed his face was more relaxed—not lined with pain the way it had been yesterday.

That was the beauty of Alonzo's violin. Even though he was gone, he still had the power to bring peace to the world.

That afternoon, Sir received an unexpected call. He quickly stepped out of the room to keep from distracting her while he answered it. When he returned a few minutes later he looked annoyed.

"My client in Marghera needs me to arrive a day earlier than planned."

"Where is Marghera?"

He gave her a mischievous grin. "I had plans to mix a bit of business with pleasure while we were in Italy. Marghera happens to be next to Venezia. I made special arrangements with Dante before we left for Russia."

"Venice?" Brie smiled, now understanding why Sir had brought the mask with him on this short excursion.

"Do you have to leave now?" Brie asked in concern.

"Unfortunately, it's urgent."

She frowned. "What about tonight with Alonzo's friends?"

He put his arms around her. "I hate that you have to meet them alone, but I need you to glean as much as you can from them. You are not just doing it for your documentary, but for me as well."

She looked up at him with compassion. "I understand."

Cradling her face in his hand, he told her, "You are my one constant—my north star."

Touched by his declaration, Brie wrapped her arms around him, holding him tight. While they stayed in that embrace, she poured every ounce of her love into him.

When Sir finally broke away, he was all business. "I'll speak with Gino and explain the situation. The only thing I want you to concentrate on is your research. I have no idea when we will have the chance to return."

She sighed, knowing this might be her only chance for a very long time.

"As far as Nonna is concerned," he continued, "I came across something today I need to investigate further. I'm hoping it will provide us with the answers we are looking for."

"I hope so too, Sir."

Brie remained in the study the entire day, working tirelessly to document as much as she could with the short amount of time she had left. She was grateful that Anthony was in the room with her because nursing him provided her with much-needed breaks throughout the day.

She was so focused on her work that it came as an unwelcome surprise when she heard a knock on the door. Glancing at her phone, she whimpered when she realized how much time had passed.

Looking sadly at the piles she still had left to go through, Brie dutifully picked up Anthony. Heading toward the door, she mentally prepared herself for the evening ahead, reminding herself how important it was to Sir.

It was a pleasant shock when she found Gino standing in the hallway to greet her. He was dressed in a fine suit, looking exceedingly professional.

"I trust your research has gone well today?"

She smiled, then glanced back at the room. "It seems there's never enough time."

"Don't concern yourself. It isn't going anywhere," he assured her.

"Do I have enough time to freshen up?"

"Of course, *bella donna*. As the guest of honor, you are allowed to be late."

She giggled. As a sub, being late was never an option. "It won't take me long, I promise."

Brie hurried to her room, happy she had thought to include a simple black dress when she packed. Although it couldn't match the formal look of Gino's attire, it fit the Italian aesthetic of understated elegance.

Brushing out her long hair, she applied a minimal amount of makeup, making sure to emphasize her eyes and lips just as she had been taught at the Training Center. After a spritz of perfume, she felt prepared to meet Alonzo's friends.

After quickly changing Anthony into fresh clothes, Brie headed to the door.

Gino's eyes shone with approval as he held out his arm to her. "*Bellissima.*"

His simple compliment filled Brie with confidence as she took his arm and walked with him down the hallway. Gino had mentioned inviting a few friends, so she was surprised to find a room full of people waiting for her.

As soon as she entered, the guests quieted. Brie scanned the room and quickly realized there were no women, only men. She turned to Gino, looking at him questioningly.

Before she could say anything, Gino addressed the crowd. "It is my pleasure to present to you Alonzo's grandson."

The entire room broke out in enthusiastic applause. One by one, each man walked up to Brie and handed her a gift for the baby, while Gino made formal introductions.

Each of them congratulated her on the birth of a healthy son and shared how they knew Alonzo. It immediately became clear that these were not Alonzo's personal friends but professional acquaintances.

Although Brie spent a pleasant evening listening to their personal stories about Alonzo's many performances all over the world, she failed to learn anything of relevance that she hadn't already learned from watching the videotapes herself.

She would have considered the evening a loss except for the conversation she had with Gino after the guests had all left. He'd invited her to sit by the fire and take a moment to reflect on the evening before she jumped back into her research.

"Thank you for your graciousness tonight, Brianna. You and your son have lifted the spirits of countless people."

Brie smiled as she stared at the fire, her spirit soothed by its dancing flames. "It was a pleasure to meet people who knew Alonzo personally."

"I don't mean to pry, Brianna, but several people asked if you will be having Anthony christened while you are here. They hoped they might be allowed to attend if that is the case."

Brie frowned and let out a troubled sigh.

"Did my question upset you?"

"No, Gino," she assured him. "We've been considering it, but Anthony's godfather can't attend." She turned to him, admitting, "It leaves us at a loss as to what to do."

"If that is the only thing stopping you, I would be honored to act as his proxy."

She looked at him in disbelief. "I didn't realize that was even an option."

"Of course," he chuckled lightly. "In today's modern world, it happens more often than you think."

Brie felt a surge of relief. "I'll speak to Thane about it."

"Please do. I would be happy to make the arrangements as well, if he would like. With my connections, I have some pull and can make that happen despite the short notice."

She felt as if a huge weight had been lifted off her shoulders knowing they now had a viable option if Sir wanted to honor Nonna's wishes.

Brie stared at the fire in silence, wanting to return to her research without appearing rude.

"Would you like to return to the study?" Gino asked.

She laughed. "Actually, I would."

Gesturing to the door, he told her, "Feel free to leave."

"You won't be offended?"

He raised an eyebrow. "I am a man who appreciates

diligence."

Brie immediately stood up, cradling Anthony against her shoulder. "Thank you, Gino. For everything."

He nodded. "Don't forget these." He pointed to the stack of envelopes containing gifts for the baby.

Brie smiled back at him as she was leaving. Returning to the study, Brie felt a sense of renewed hope as she stared at the pile of envelopes on the table. They represented the love people felt not only for the baby but for Alonzo himself.

Although Brie had initially considered the evening a waste of her time, she realized now that those connections would become important to her in the future when she released the documentary about Alonzo's life.

Her thoughts were interrupted when her phone alerted her to a text. Brie smiled when she saw it was from Sir, but then her heart skipped a beat when she read it.

Call me. I have important news to share about Nonna.

Verity

B rie was on pins and needles as she dialed the phone to call Sir, wondering what he had discovered.

"Hey, babygirl. I found out some disturbing news about Nonna."

Brie felt her stomach twist into a knot. "What is it Sir?" she asked, her hand shaking as she held onto the phone.

"You have to understand that my grandparents have never left the island, so there are municipal records dating back to when they first got married. Through Portoferraio's online records, I came across certificates that document a history of miscarriages. My grandmother suffered two miscarriages before my father was born, and then suffered four more after his birth."

"Poor Nonna."

"That's not the worst of it. She lost her last child during birth. That death was the reason Alonzo quit the tour and returned home."

Brie broke down crying, remembering how close

they had been to losing Hope and Anthony during childbirth. She could only imagine the devastation Nonna must have felt. "Oh, Sir…"

"The pain she must have endured when their only child committed suicide years later…" Sir said, his voice breaking with sorrow.

Brie sank to the floor, clutching the phone, her heart breaking for Nonna. "The unbearable loss she must feel."

"I understand why my grandfather is so protective of her," Sir stated gruffly.

"He lost them, too," Brie whimpered.

"They have both suffered immense loss, but I suspect Nonna has always blamed herself."

It crushed Brie to think Nonna had spent her life grieving those tragedies in silence and shame. "My heart breaks for Nonna."

"I am not a man moved to tears, but I have shed many for her today."

Wiping away her own tears, Brie asked, "What can we do for her?"

"I have given it some thought. When we return, I'm going to share what I've learned, and you and I will give her whatever support she needs."

"What about the christening, Sir?"

"I am still undecided. What are your thoughts?"

"Tonight, several of Alonzo's friends asked if the baby was going to be christened before we leave Italy. Gino mentioned that he would be willing to stand in as Rytsar's proxy."

"Proxy…I hadn't considered that," Sir muttered.

"However, christenings are scheduled months before a child's birth. It may not be an option even if we decided to move forward with it."

"Sir, he also offered to set up the arrangements and mentioned he has some pull."

"I bet he does," he snorted. "Well, at least that gives us options. We'll talk more about it tomorrow night."

"Tomorrow?"

"Yes. The issue up here, although unexpected, has been easily resolved and should be concluded by my meeting tomorrow afternoon. Which means you'll be joining me in Venice in the evening."

Brie trembled, remembering how incredible her last time in Venice had been.

In a more serious tone, he told her, "I would like to leave the following morning to return to my grandparents."

She glanced at the boxes and materials scattered throughout the room, resigned to the fact that she would not be able to finish her research. Although she'd hoped for more time, it would have to wait.

Family was more important.

Gino came to speak with Brie the next morning, informing her that Sir had requested his driver leave in the early afternoon for Venice and she should be ready to go by then.

He smiled when he saw her distraught look. "It is as

I said before, *bella donna.* The boxes will be waiting for you when you return."

"I just wish I knew when that would be," she laughed, rocking Anthony in her arms.

Gino told her with a smirk, "The future is hard to predict unless you happen to be God."

She smiled. By way of thanks, Brie held out the baby to him. "Would you like to hold him one more time, Gino?"

"Certainly." He took Anthony and held him as stiffly as he had the first time. Looking down at her tiny son, he declared, "Anthony Alonzo Davis, you will become a great man someday and fulfill your grandfather's destiny."

Brie saw tears in his eyes when he handed Anthony back to her.

"My offer stands concerning the christening," he reminded her. "I simply need the day and time, and I will arrange it for you."

"Thane and I are still discussing it," she explained.

He nodded. "I am at your disposal if you need me."

"Thank you, Gino."

Brie felt a surge of nervous exhilaration when he took her hand and brought it to his lips, kissing it gently. "*A risentirci.*"

She nodded, blushing unexpectedly. Gino Mancini exuded confidence on a level that dwarfed most men, and she found it quite disconcerting.

Hours later, Gino saw her off personally, instructing his driver to be careful on the road, "Their lives are priceless to me."

"Understood, Signore Mancini," his driver replied. Looking back at Brie from the front seat, he nodded curtly.

The man did not speak the entire drive, his attention focused solely on the road before him.

She didn't mind his silence. The beautiful Italian countryside with its large vineyards, old farmhouses, and the occasional castle was truly a feast for the eyes. The fact that she was headed to Venice to meet Sir, made the drive even more enjoyable.

Brie immediately recognized the young man with wavy brown hair waiting for her at the train station. "Dante!"

He flashed her a smile and walked over to them. Nodding to Gino's driver, he said with a tone of authority, "She's under my care now, Leone."

"Very well," the man answered, handing Dante her luggage and baby carrier before getting into his vehicle without another word to Brie.

"Follow me, Signora Davis," Dante told her with a glint in his eye. "Your husband has planned an extravagant evening for you."

Once they were on the train that would take them on the short ride over the water to Venice, she gushed, "Dante, I know I've said it before, but the mask you made…it is the most beautiful thing I've ever seen. I still can't believe you created it especially for me."

He smiled, and said with pride in his eyes, "My muses were truly inspired, *signora*."

Brie suddenly thought of the notes on the mask and asked him, "Those music notes…did those come from a song by chance?"

He gave her an amused smile. "Your husband asked me the same question, so I'll tell you what I told him. I believe they are on a music sheet in one of the boxes you and I were going through at my godfather's, but I can't be certain."

Brie sighed, knowing it must have been frustrating for Sir to hear that. "Wherever they came from, your mask is a true piece of art. It belongs in a museum, not on my face."

"I wholeheartedly disagree, Signora Davis. It was specifically made for your face, and it will be my honor tonight to see it properly displayed."

Brie felt the heat of a blush rise to her cheeks.

Dante gazed at her son and grinned. "The last time we spoke, you only had a *bambina*."

Brie looked down at Anthony, laughing. "It turns out Mr. Davis and I are quite compatible."

He chuckled. "I can see that."

Curious, she asked him, "Do you know who will be watching my son this evening?"

"My sister," Dante answered proudly. "Giana has four children of her own, but they are mostly grown now, so she is looking forward to caring for a little one again."

It warmed Brie's heart to know that Dante's family would be caring for him. "Do you know how long the event tonight will be?"

"That is up to the partners involved," he answered with a glint in his eye.

She smiled, remembering her honeymoon and the

Venetian party where she met Dante. It had ended earlier than expected because Sir had been unable to control his passion for her.

Brie would never forget how he released that passion in the most sinfully erotic way on the streets of Venice.

Dante took Brie to a hotel overlooking the canals of Venice. When she entered the room, she found a gown laid out on the bed for her. "Your husband instructed me to tell you to dress and wait for your escort."

"You're not my escort?" she asked in surprise.

He smiled mischievously. "No, but I will be seeing you at the event."

After he was gone, Brie walked through the room, delighted by Sir's choice of hotel. The room was decorated with the clean look of white furniture and marble, while colorful Venetian masks accented the walls—each one unique and timeless.

She lay down on the chaise lounge by the window to look out at the busy canal while she nursed Anthony. Brie smiled as she watched the sky light up with pink, orange, and blue as the sun slowly set over the ancient city.

It amazed Brie to think how the beauty she was witnessing was commonplace for those who lived here. She could understand why Dante was inspired by Venice and its people.

Once Anthony's tummy was full and he was content,

Brie picked up the dress Sir had chosen for her. The silk dress was the color of champagne and felt luxurious to the touch. Brie noticed that high heels, but no underwear, had been provided. She took that as Sir's preference.

After taking a quick shower to freshen up, she slid the simple dress over her head and purred as it slipped over her naked skin.

Spying the sapphire box, Brie smiled as she opened the lid and lifted the mask with reverence, stunned by its intricate beauty. The delicate mask covered in sparkling crystals had a violin on the upper right side made of amber stones. On the left were black jewels that made up the five musical notes. Dante had placed the pattern of notes on a staff that was wavy rather than straight, giving the notes a feeling of movement.

Brie walked up to the mirror and placed it over her eyes. The mask's feminine shape was contoured to her face, and the color of the violin and notes enhanced the honey color of her eyes. No makeup was needed, so Brie kept it simple, not wanting to distract from the beauty of the mask itself.

After styling her hair and slipping her heels on, there was nothing left to do but sit and take in the view of the city below. While it bustled with activity during the day, Venice took on a much different feel at night. It became quiet and mysterious as darkness settled over it.

When Brie heard a knock at the door, she hurried to answer it and found two people standing there. The first she realized must be Dante's sister. She had the same wavy brown hair and smile.

The other was an intriguing stranger. He wore a

black mask similar to hers in that it had the same five notes on the left. He was dressed in a dark gray suit, but no tie. Instead, the collar of his dress shirt was left unbuttoned, showing off just a hint of his chest hair. It was subtle but quite alluring.

"Signora Davis," the man said in a deep voice. She nodded, conscious of his appraising gaze as he looked her over.

The woman smiled. "I've come to care for your son." Holding out her hand, she said, "My name is Giana, I'm—"

"Dante's sister," Brie finished, shaking her hand warmly. "Please come in, both of you."

While Brie introduced Giana to her son, the man who had come to escort her to the party stood by the window, silently observing her. It was both flustering and arousing to be watched so closely by a stranger.

After giving Giana simple instructions, Brie went to grab her purse.

The man stopped her, pulling an envelope from his breast pocket and handing it to her.

Breaking the seal, she took out the note and smiled when she recognized Sir's exquisite handwriting.

Giovanni is your escort tonight. Do not speak a word until we meet. Chest out, exude elegance and poise, and be confident in the knowledge you are mine.

~Thane

Shivers of excitement coursed through her as she

read her Master's instructions. Looking up at Giovanni, she nodded in understanding. He then took the mask from the box and stood behind her as he placed it over her eyes. Securing it in place, he slowly turned her around. He shook his head in disbelief as he looked at her, and let out an appreciative whistle.

"Oh!" Giana gasped, putting her hand to her mouth. "Dante outdid himself. It is exquisite." She looked at Brie in wonder. "You're exquisite."

Brie smiled graciously.

Giovanni held his arm out to Brie, a look of veneration in his eyes. It was exhilarating!

She glanced at her son as Giana picked him up. "Anthony will be well cared for until your husband instructs me to return," she assured Brie.

Nodding to her, Brie turned to face Giovanni and took his arm. They walked out into the dark streets of Venice, which were illuminated by the romantic light of the streetlamps. Brie remembered when Sir told her that the most romantic city in the world also happened to be one of the kinkiest.

The few people wandering the streets gave her admiring glances as she walked past them. She ate up the attention with the confidence that came from being Sir's beloved submissive.

When Giovanni walked up to the quaint apartment with the vibrant green door and knocked on it three times, then paused before knocking twice more, Brie couldn't help but smile.

There was no turning back now from the kinkiness about to ensue.

The Mask

Giovanni looked at Brie and brushed a stray hair from her face as they waited at the door. The simple touch felt intimate and she blushed.

"You are stunning," he stated in a low masculine voice that made her tremble. "Almost too beautiful to touch."

She smiled on hearing his unusual compliment.

A young woman answered the door and stood staring at Brie for a moment before stepping to the side and bowing to them both. "Please come inside."

It was amazing to Brie the power Dante's mask seemed to have over people!

Giovanni nodded to the young lady as they walked into the room, and their hostess shut the door behind them. Placing his hand on the small of Brie's back, he escorted her up the long flight of stairs. Brie could hear the festivities were already underway and wondered how many people were attending tonight.

Her first time here, Brie had known almost no Italian. This time would be different, which made the evening even more exciting for her.

When they reached the top of the stairs, she found it crowded with people. She spotted Dante first, talking to a group of people while he casually sipped a glass of wine.

A man beside her announced to the room, "Presenting Brianna Davis, wife of Thane Davis, the esteemed son of Alonzo Davis, and her escort, Giovanni Bernardi."

The entire room turned to look and hushed as Giovanni walked Brie into the room. The expression on Dante's face was euphoric. He looked as if he were experiencing a sacred vision. "*Divina…*"

The others in the room muttered quietly in agreement.

Their unexpected reaction would have been embarrassing for Brie had it not been for the man standing in the back staring at her.

Sir's possessive stare gave her butterflies. Unlike the others in the room, he *knew* her heart belonged only to him.

Dante walked up to Brie, shaking his head in wonder. "The mask suits you far better than I ever dreamed, *signora*. You are perfection."

When she looked into Dante's brown eyes to thank him, she immediately noticed that he, too, wore a black mask with golden notes, just like Giovanni. "Your mask has stolen everyone's breath away," she told him, giggling lightly.

Dante took her hand and kissed it. "It is you, *signora*.

The mask is merely an accessory."

She smiled when she corrected him. "I'm the accessory, Dante. The mask is the star."

"I humbly disagree," Sir stated as he approached. "The mask complements you. It is *not* the other way around."

She blushed under her Master's high praise, pleased to see that he was also wearing a black mask with gold notes. At the first party, Dante had been the only one to wear a mask that matched hers, leaving Brie to suspect that this evening she would be enjoying the attention of several men.

"Would you like a glass of red wine, téa?"

"Yes, Master. Thank you."

Sir nodded to someone behind her.

While everyone else's eyes were still on her, Brie's gaze was locked on Sir's. His black suit, combined with the sexy mask he wore, gave her a hint of a *Phantom of the Opera* vibe, which she found quite alluring.

"For you, beautiful lady."

Brie turned to see an older gentleman with a beard handing her a glass of wine. To her surprise, he also wore a black mask with golden notes.

"*Grazie,*" she murmured, looking back at Sir.

Brie glanced at his mask again, and then at each of the other men. She finally made the connection that, for tonight's party, the notes represented each man and she was the fifth note.

Clever Sir…

A beautiful chime sounded at the other end of the room, announcing the beginning of the event. People began pairing up based on their matching masks. They moved gracefully across the floor as they met up with their partner for the evening.

Brie, however, was already surrounded by the four men she would be scening with.

"Are you ready for a night you will never forget, téa?" Sir asked, holding out his hand to her.

Her heart skipped a beat as she took it.

Sir led her to the next room, her entourage of admiring men following behind her. It was decorated in luxurious shades of purple that contrasted beautifully with the golden chaise lounge set in the middle of the room.

"I will undress her," Sir told the three men as he grazed Brie's arm with his fingers. Goosebumps rose on her skin, her body responding to the electricity of her Master's touch.

Leaning in close, he whispered, "I want you to concentrate on each man's caress as they explore your body tonight. They are allowed to touch but *not* to take what is mine."

"Oh…" she gasped, excited by his command. The moment his lips descended on her throat, Brie's pussy ached with need for him.

While the other men watched, Sir slowly pulled her dress up to her thighs, teasing them as he lifted the material to expose her ass and bare pussy. She heard Giovanni growl under his breath.

There was something incredibly arousing about being the center of their attention when they knew they could not have her.

It took the experience to another level, just as it had on her honeymoon when she'd been part of this private community and explored the connection with others through touch. However, this time, instead of tempting just one man, she was tempting many.

Sir continued to lift her dress, sliding the silken material over her stomach and stopping just under her breasts. Her nipples were hard, and she enjoyed the gentle friction the soft material caused. Turning her head to expose her neck, he bit down on her throat as he lifted the dress over her breasts, baring them to the men.

She heard their grunts of approval as Sir took one breast in his hand and squeezed it lightly. "They want you, téa. Shall we give them a taste?"

Sir pulled the dress off and told her to turn slowly for them, wanting them to see every inch of her body. He then laid her on the chaise lounge and instructed her to arch her back and open her legs to them.

Raising her breasts in the air with her pussy dripping in excitement, she lay there waiting. Sir took his time, letting her savor this moment before he commanded them to join her.

Sir knelt on the floor by her head, claiming her lips for himself, which left the rest of her body for the other men to explore. Brie recognized Dante's light touch first and moaned softly when he grazed her nipple with his palm, causing a jolt of electricity that traveled straight to her groin.

Giovanni's touch was more commanding. He grabbed her other breast possessively and began teasing her nipple with his thumb. She enjoyed the contrast between the two caresses and purred with pleasure.

Her bearded partner was a distinguished gentleman with a quiet but forceful dominance. He slowly traced his fingers over her stomach, leaving her skin tingling as he trailed his hand down to her bare mound. Groaning when he felt the extent of her excitement, he began teasing her sensitive clit.

"While you focus on their touch," Sir whispered huskily, "I want you to respond to it. There is no need for control tonight, my dear; only unrestrained enjoyment."

When he kissed her again, Brie returned the kiss, expressing her love and appreciation. To be at the center of four skilled Dominant's attention with no other expectations than to enjoy it…?

That was pure submissive bliss.

Obeying Sir's command, Brie focused on each man's unique touch. Dante's caresses reminded her of a young lover touching the object of his romantic obsession. His touches were reverent, passionate, and all-consuming.

Giovanni was a more demanding lover, wanting to possess her body as he reveled in it. Brie's heart raced as he sucked, nibbled, and grazed his teeth over her skin, wanting to taste all of her.

And then there was the man between her legs. She smiled when she felt the tickle of his beard against her inner thigh as he licked her pussy, his tongue commanding her body to succumb to his pleasure as he skillfully brought her to the edge.

When her first orgasm hit, all four men groaned, turned on by her physical pleasure.

Dante ripped off his shirt, utilizing the intimate contact that naked skin provided. His bare chest sported six-pack abs and a sexy V-line. That V-line drew her eyes to the hardness of his shaft straining against his pants.

Giovanni also rid himself of his shirt. He had an abundance of chest hair and hard muscles that flexed when he moved back into position. His mouth claimed her nipple as he reached down for her pussy.

Her bearded partner allowed Giovanni access to her clit while he unbuttoned his shirt, showing off his salt and pepper chest hair. He stared at her lustfully as he slowly slipped his finger inside her wet pussy and began teasing her G-spot, while Giovanni vigorously rubbed her clit.

Brie threw back her head and moaned, embracing the sexual energy building inside her. Erotic sounds of pleasure rose up as each couple around them explored the heightened pleasure touch could inspire.

Then Brie heard Sir unzip his pants. "Take my cock into your mouth, téa."

Still wearing her mask, she eagerly grasped his shaft and tilted her head back, parting her lips for him. Her whole body shuddered in ecstasy when he penetrated her mouth with his cock, and she quickly came again.

There was something extraordinarily erotic knowing Sir was watching the other men tease her body while he pleasured himself with her mouth. Each of them played their part in this amorous dance of carnal desire.

Brie's muffle cry signaled another climax that had snuck up on her. Her entire body trembled while she remained in that heightened state, orgasming multiple times. Her bearded partner lifted his head from between her legs, a ravenous look in his eyes as he wiped his mouth. "*Deliziosa.*"

Brie continued to suck her Master's cock while the three men took turns eating her pussy. While one man was busy, the others explored her body with their hands, teeth, and lips.

Sir abruptly pulled away at one point and picked up her dress, motioning to Dante. Leaning in close, Sir told her from between clenched teeth, "I am too close to the edge."

The other two men helped Brie to her feet while Dante quickly dressed her.

"Thank your partners," Sir replied gruffly.

Brie could barely stand on her own, riding on the high of multiple orgasms. Turning to Dante first, she bowed graciously, "Thank you, Dante."

He took her hand and lifted it to his lips, saying her name in his sexy Italian accent, "Brianna."

She turned to Giovanni next. He too took her hand and kissed it when she thanked him. "My pleasure, Signora Davis."

Facing her last partner, Brie asked him, "What is your name?"

"Leonardo," he answered in a low, deep voice.

The man's beard smelled of her, which she found erotically charming. "Thank you, Leonardo."

He lifted her hand, kissing it with reverence, his eyes burning with unfulfilled desire. "*Ciao, bella.*"

Sir put his hand around Brie's waist and nodded to the three men. He walked out with her, his gate stiffer than usual. Once they were back on the streets, Sir swept her off her feet and started carrying her.

She giggled. "Where are you taking me?"

"To be fucked."

Sir was a man on a mission, scouting the area as he walked. When he found a darkened alleyway that led to the water, he headed down it. At the end of the alley, a marble statue of a lion glowed in the moonlight.

Setting her on the statue's pedestal, Sir began kissing her ravenously. The hunger in each kiss stole her breath away as his lips bruised hers with his unbridled passion.

Throwing caution to the wind, Sir hurriedly lifted her dress and unzipped his pants. Clutching her hips with both hands, he covered her mouth with his to muffle her cries when he thrust into her.

Lost in the heat of his raging need for release, Brie grabbed him, forcing him even deeper. His primal grunts filled the air as he gave in to his lust, fucking his masked submissive on the streets of Venice under a starry night.

It was a sexual masterpiece.

Priceless

That night, while Anthony lay sleeping between them, Brie caught Sir staring at her in the moonlight filtering through the window. Tingles coursed through her body just thinking about the evening she'd just experienced.

He reached out to stroke her cheek. "I needed tonight."

"You were a true artist, Sir."

Looking into her eyes, he confessed, "Tonight was as much for me as it was for you."

"How so?" She was surprised to hear his admission when the entire scene had been so focused on her.

He cleared his throat, suddenly overcome with emotion. "I was desperate for the distraction."

She looked at him sadly. "I'm sorry you've had so much to deal with."

He frowned. "When Nonna asked what my father's death was like, it set off an army of demons in my head. Looking through his things has only made it worse, and

176

then…to learn about the tragedies my grandmother has suffered. It's almost been too much."

She nodded, tears coming to her eyes.

"And, yet, I will be strong for her tomorrow. Nonna deserves no less. Which…is why tonight was important. I was desperate for a release." He looked at her thoughtfully. "However, I'm concerned I may have been too rough."

She shook her head. "Never, Sir. It was perfect. You are perfect."

He snorted. "I am far from perfect."

"You are perfect for me," she countered.

Leaning over Anthony, Sir kissed her lightly on the lips. "Keep telling yourself that, babygirl."

She laughed softly, cherishing the quiet moment with him.

"What are your honest thoughts on the christening?" he asked, glancing down at Anthony.

"If it brings Nonna some peace, and Rytsar is okay with it, I think we should."

Sir nodded. "I feel the same as you." Reaching over to the side table, he grabbed his phone and dialed Rytsar's number.

Brie could hear the Russian's laughter when he answered, "Having trouble sleeping, *moy droog?*"

Putting him on speaker, Sir replied, "We have a serious question for you."

"Shoot."

Brie spoke up, "Would you be okay if we do Anthony's christening with a proxy? Nonna would like us to do it before we leave here."

Sir added, "She has been quite insistent about it. I believe it would bring her peace."

Rytsar took a few moments before he answered. "Your grandmother is a good woman, brother. I would not stand in the way of her peace."

Brie was touched by his kindness. "I love you!"

He chuckled warmly. "And I love you, *radost moya*. However, I do have a request."

"What's that?" Sir asked him.

"Make sure the proxy is worthy to stand in my stead. I don't want a wuss representing Anthony's *dyadya*."

Brie giggled.

"Certainly, old friend." Sir paused for a moment before adding, "Thank you."

"Of course, *moy droog*. Wait. I do have another request."

Sir chuckled. "Fine, what is it?"

"I'm serious about number three."

Without hesitating, Sir hung up on him.

Brie laughed loudly enough to stir Anthony and had to cover her mouth until he settled again.

Sir's eyes glinted in the moonlight, amused by her laughter. "You make my world a better place, Mrs. Davis."

She smiled lovingly at him. "I feel the same, Mr. Davis."

They started the next morning on a much more somber

note as they prepared to return to Isola d'Elba.

Although Brie was excited about seeing Hope again and trusted that the time spent with her grandparents had helped ease Nonna's heart, Brie knew that today would be difficult for both Sir and his grandmother.

Sir withdrew into himself as he drove. Brie understood his need for silence and spent the four-hour drive admiring the changing countryside while caring for their son.

The ferry ride to Portoferraio was a welcomed break for Brie. She watched as Sir stood on the deck by himself, looking out at the ocean, the wind whipping through his hair. She knew the ocean held a special place in Sir's heart because of its connection with his father, but she was uncertain if it was providing comfort or was only a source of pain for him now.

Aunt Fortuna was eagerly waiting for them at the port. She started telling them about all the fun adventures Hope had been on while they were gone. But she quickly picked up that things were not okay with Sir and whispered to Brie, "What happened?"

Brie answered simply, "Sir needs to speak with Nonna."

Aunt Fortuna looked stricken. "Please intervene, Brianna. Thane and the great-grandchildren are all she has left."

Brie assured her, "Sir loves Nonna."

Aunt Fortuna glanced back at Sir, still concerned, but nodded to her.

Brie was unsure how Sir would broach the subject with his grandmother, but she should have known he would be direct. As soon as they arrived at the apartment, he said, "Nonna, we need to talk."

Nonna's face went pale the moment she heard the serious tone in his voice, and she quickly grabbed the chair beside her for support. "What about, *Nipotino?*"

His grandfather instantly became defensive and warned Sir, "I will not let you hurt her."

Sir opened his hands wide to show Nonno he meant no harm. "I simply want to talk with her—alone."

His grandfather shot a worried glance at Nonna, clearly uncomfortable with Sir's request.

"Take Brianna with you when you talk!" Aunt Fortuna cried out.

Sir looked at Brie for a moment, then turned to Nonna. "I leave that up to you."

"I would like Brianna to stay."

Nonno caressed his wife's cheek. "I will be outside, Rosanna. Call from the balcony if you need me."

Nonna gave him a nervous smile, pressing her forehead against his. "*Ti amo molto,*" she whispered. Brie could hear the fear in her voice.

Aunt Fortuna took the baby from Brie, while Nonno grabbed Hope's hand and slowly walked her down the stairs. Once the apartment was silent, Sir asked Nonna to sit.

His grandmother wrung her hands nervously, glancing at Brie while she waited for Sir to speak.

"I..." Sir stood up and began pacing the floor. "I'll just be blunt." Turning to Nonna, he said, "I know about all the children you've lost."

She stared at him as if she had no idea what he was

talking about.

"There is no reason to hide it, Nonna," he said gently. "There never was."

She shook her head and said curtly, "I do not know what you are talking about."

Sir walked up and sat down beside her. "I'm talking about the miscarriages and the stillbirth."

Nonna stared at him, wide-eyed, looking as if he had stabbed her in the chest with a knife.

Sir put an arm around her as tears ran down his cheeks. "I'm so sorry, Nonna."

Her bottom lip began to tremble as she watched his tears in disbelief. Still, she kept her silence.

Then, as if a dam suddenly broke inside her, a heart-wrenching wail escaped her lips. It was the chilling cry of a mother who had lost a child—the kind of sound that rips out the heart of anyone near enough to hear it.

Sir gathered Nonna in his arms and held her tight as years of pent-up grief bubbled to the surface. Brie instinctively joined him, hugging Nonna, wanting to build an emotional wall of protection around her. Brie knew such all-consuming grief had the frightening power to obliterate a person.

It hurt Brie to hear Sir's heartfelt sobs while he grieved with his grandmother over her babies who never took a breath of life. Nonna clutched him as she rode out her grief, quieting one moment and screaming the next as she cried out the names of the babies she never got to hold.

At one point, Brie caught Nonno standing at the top of the stairs, desperate to check on his wife. When he saw Nonna was safe in Sir's arms, he nodded to Brie and quietly left.

Hours later, her grief had finally abated enough for her to talk. Nonna let go of Sir.

Looking completely spent, she found the strength to ask Sir in a voice hoarse with grief, "Who told you?"

"No one. Your losses were recorded in the municipal archives."

She looked down at her withered hands, shaking her head sadly.

"You have every right to grieve, Nonna. There was no reason to hide it from me—from anyone."

She swallowed hard. "I am a mother with no living children. You cannot know how that feels, *Nipotino*."

She glanced up at Brie, "And I pray to God every day you never have to."

"Oh, Nonna," Brie wept, her heart breaking all over again.

Nonna turned to Sir and asked hesitantly, "*Nipotino*?"

"Yes, Nonna?" he said, squeezing her hand.

"I need to know…"

Sir winced as he finished her sentence, "About his death?"

She gazed into his eyes, the tears starting to fall again. "Please."

Sir stood up and began pacing again. Brie could tell he was struggling, wanting to give his grandmother what she needed, but not wanting to open himself up to all of the pain associated with his father's death.

After several minutes, Sir finally dragged a chair over to Nonna and sat across from her. Brie held her breath when he gently took his grandmother's hands in his.

"After he shot himself…"

Sir closed his eyes for a moment, before starting again.

"After he shot himself, he was remorseful." Sir choked up when he said, "Papa told me he loved me."

Nonna nodded slowly, unable to speak as tears rained down her gaunt cheeks.

Sir gazed into her eyes. He looked as if his heart was about to break. "His very last words were 'I'm sorry.'"

Nonna sucked in a sharp breath and started rocking back and forth, sobbing to herself, "My poor boy…"

After several minutes, Sir squeezed her hands again. "Nonna."

When she met his gaze, he told her, "I believe he died still wanting to live. He did not want this for you—for us."

She took Sir's face in her trembling hands, the expression on her face unbearably sad as she pressed her forehead against his and said in a ragged whisper. "Oh, *Nipotino*…"

No one could know the pain they shared without having lived it themselves. So, Brie stayed where she was beside Nonna, silently sending her strength to them both, unable to stop the tears that streamed down her face.

On a cold winter's day, Brie walked up the hill to the

church Nonno and Nonna had attended since they were children. It was the very same church that Sir's father and Sir himself had been christened in.

Unlike Hope's christening, where Sir's entire family had attended, as well as Brie's parents, the only ones joining them on this day were Nonno and Nonna, Aunt Fortuna, and Gino Mancini—the man acting as Rytsar's proxy.

It was a formal occasion and was given the same pageantry as Hope's christening, despite the small assembly of people gathered to witness it.

Gino reverently took Anthony from Brie's arms. He kept the time-honored tradition of not looking back when he walked up to present their son to the priest, wanting to ensure their child would grow up strong, courageous, and without fear.

Brie stood proudly beside Sir, who was holding Hope. Their little girl was fascinated by everything inside the church and kept pointing at the colorful stained-glass windows, saying, "Pretty!"

Brie smiled at her, loving her daughter's innocent enthusiasm.

Glancing at Nonna, Brie's smile grew even wider. Nonna wore a look of pure joy as the priest poured the holy water over Anthony's head and blessed him.

Sir winked at Brie, both of them content in their decision. To bring Nonna this moment of happiness, a woman who had suffered greatly but who had also been a blessing to so many, was priceless.

Kaylee

After the whirlwind travel, Brie found she was grateful to return to California. As wonderful and exciting as the trip had been, there was something about the comfort of home that called to her soul.

There was no other place like it in the world.

While Brie was unpacking the next morning, she came across the sapphire box. Memories of her night in Venice came flooding back, and Brie decided to hang it up in the bedroom rather than keep the museum-worthy mask tucked away for safekeeping. It deserved to be on display and would remind her of the scene Sir so carefully crafted for her.

Sir had driven to downtown LA for a business meeting, leaving her a day to herself. Stacking all of the notes on her desk that she and Sir had taken while at Gino's, Brie started matching the letters with the timing of each recorded concert so that she could better understand the progression of Alonzo's music as it related to his personal life. She wanted to do it while it was still fresh in her mind.

Brie felt teary when she came across Alonzo's letter informing Gino he was dropping out of his tour to return home to his mother. Since the recent revelation, she now knew Nonna had been grieving the death of a child at the time. Alonzo's decision to risk his career to return home testified to the kind of man he was, as well as the level of commitment he had to his family. Brie respected him for that decision and was grateful Alonzo's blood flowed through Sir's veins.

With Anthony on the floor beside her, snuggled in the infant carrier so she could rock him with her foot, and Hope playing with Shadow in her office, Brie felt ready to dive into her work.

Before she could begin, however, Mary called. "You better get your ass here now," she told Brie, her voice tense.

"What's wrong?" Brie was terrified something bad had happened to her.

"I'm at Marquis Gray's house. Kylie's parents have come to take the child."

Brie's heart dropped. The last thing Faelan needed was to lose custody of his daughter now. It would completely derail him.

Since she had no time to get a sitter, Brie bundled her children into the car and headed straight to Marquis Gray's home. It seemed strange that Mary should be there, but then Brie remembered that Candy told her that Mary had made a point to visit Faelan's daughter regularly while he was in Russia. Unable to help him, she had concentrated her efforts on helping Marquis and Celestia with his baby.

Brie was surprised to see both Mary and Lea waiting for her outside the house when she pulled up.

"What took you so long?" Mary snarled.

"I came as fast as I could," Brie shot back, unbuckling Hope from her car seat.

"I did, too," Lea grumbled, taking Hope from Brie. It was obvious she'd been in the middle of yoga class by her matching purple yoga outfit and messy bun. She leaned in close. "Mary is surly as all get out, but don't let it faze you. She's just worried about the kid."

Brie glanced at Mary in concern. "Did they win custody?"

"No. Kylie's parents flew out to see the baby and are now refusing to leave without her."

"Where's Marquis Gray?"

"He's in there trying to reason with them, but they won't take no as an answer." She looked at Brie hopefully. "I figure since you just saw Faelan, you can convince them to stay the fuck away from his kid."

Mary turned to Lea. "We're just here to act as a last line of protection, in case things get too crazy."

"I'm sure we can talk this out," Brie assured Mary as she picked up Anthony and kicked the door shut.

"I wouldn't be so sure about that…" Mary chuckled ruefully as she took Anthony from Brie and opened the front door.

Brie could hear them arguing fiercely as soon as she entered the house. Mary shut the door behind her, the two of them staying outside to shield her children from the fight taking place.

Brie took a deep breath and started down the hall to the room where she could hear the raised voices. She listened to Marquis Gray respond in an even tone to the irate demands of Kylie's father.

"We're not leaving without our granddaughter!"

"As I've stated before, there is a legal protocol you must follow. You cannot have her."

"Like hell I can't! You're not even related to her. Why the hell is a stranger caring for my own flesh and blood?"

"It's not right!" Kylie's mother screamed, staring down Celestia, who was holding the crying child. "It's bad enough we've lost our daughter. How dare you keep us from our grandbaby, too! It's too much. Too much!"

Celestia took a step back when the woman tried to grab the baby from her. Marquis Gray immediately intervened, standing in front of Celestia to protect them both.

Brie stood in the doorway, frozen and unseen, unsure of what to do.

Kylie's father narrowed his eyes as he glared at Marquis Gray. "That *boy* is not fit to be her father. You know it, and I know it. Stand aside."

"I will not," Marquis Gray stated firmly.

He suddenly glanced in Brie's direction as if he wasn't surprised to see her. "Brianna Davis just came back from Russia after visiting your *son-in-law*. Why don't you ask her?"

Brie appreciated that Marquis was purposely emphasizing that Kylie's parents were still related to Faelan by marriage even though she had died.

Kylie's father immediately refocused his rage on her. "Tell me the truth," he demanded. "Todd can't even take care of himself, much less a baby. Isn't that the reason he ran away to Russia 'on business'?"

Brie shook her head. "He is part of an important project in Russia. However, he told me personally that he's returning as soon as possible so he can raise his daughter."

"What kind of man chooses work over his own child?" Kylie's mother yelled at Brie. "That just proves he is unfit to be a father."

"Todd is a good man," Celestia protested.

The woman turned on Celestia. "He let my daughter die right in front of his own eyes. He's going to do the same to our sweet grandbaby."

Chills coursed down Brie's spine. She now realized that Kylie's parents were blaming Faelan for her death.

"The medical staff did everything they could to save her!" Brie insisted. "You weren't there, I was."

"Oh, you'd say anything to protect him," the father spat. "You all would." He glared at Marquis and Celestia. "But it's to the detriment of my granddaughter, and I won't allow you to hurt her anymore."

The baby began wailing in Celestia's arms.

"Can't you see you're scaring her?" Brie cried. "All this yelling is terrifying for her."

Marquis Gray spoke again, bringing calm to the situation. "You have no legal right to take her. Until you get a ruling from the judge, Todd Wallace still has full custody of the child."

Kylie's mother suddenly slapped his face, the sound

of it echoing in the room while everyone fell silent.

Unfazed, Marquis Gray told her, "Physical assault will not be tolerated. The police will be called if you do that again."

"Give me my granddaughter!" she shouted angrily.

The moment Marquis Gray met the woman's gaze, she immediately went mute. She looked like a deer caught in the headlights.

"Don't you dare threaten my wife!" Kylie's father roared. Raging like a bull, he shoved Marquis Gray out of the way and ripped the poor baby out of Celestia's arms.

He grabbed his wife's hand and headed toward the front door.

Brie stood planted where she was with her arms spread wide, acting as a barrier.

His eyes flashed with rage as he barreled toward her. "So help me God, I'm not responsible if you get in my way."

"Stop!"

Brie was shocked to hear Faelan's voice ring out. She turned to see him behind her. He stood in the doorway like an impenetrable force, unwilling to budge.

Brie shook her head in disbelief. He didn't even look the same. Gone was the eyepatch as he stared down Kylie's father with two blue eyes and a fiery gaze that Brie had never seen before. The prosthetic looked so real, she would never have guessed it was fake.

The room became deathly silent except for the wails of the crying child.

Walking past Brie, Faelan strode up to Kylie's father

and took the crying infant from him. The moment the baby was in her father's arms, she instantly began to quiet down.

Faelan glared at the man. "No one is taking my daughter!"

Kylie's mother suddenly burst into tears. "She needs to be with us. You can't provide a stable environment for her like we can."

"I will do everything in my power to protect and provide for her."

"That's not enough," she exclaimed. "The child needs to be loved."

Faelan looked down at his daughter, his expression becoming tender. "She's a part of Kylie. Of course I will love her."

"We don't trust you," Kylie's father growled. "You've been an absentee father since the day she was born."

Faelan looked up at him and frowned. "I lost the love of my life. I'm allowed time to grieve her death."

Kylie's mother let out a strangled sob.

"Don't think we don't grieve for Kylie every damn day," her father snarled.

"And you should. She was an incredible woman," Faelan stated, rocking the baby in his arms.

"Why the sudden change of heart?" her father challenged.

Faelan looked into his eyes. "I have you to thank for that."

"Me?"

"I understand your desire to care for your grandchild, but it is not your place. Kylie would want me to raise our daughter."

"You can't know that," he insisted.

"Yes, I can. I feel it here with every heartbeat." Faelan placed a hand over his heart.

Looking back down at the tiny child in his arms, he made a vow. "Kaylee Grace Wallace, I promise before God and everyone present, to love and respect you for the rest of my life. I will guide and comfort you until the day I get the honor of giving you away to the person you deem worthy of your love."

Brie stared at him in awe, touched by his declaration.

"I still don't trust you," Kylie's father grumbled.

Brie's jaw dropped when Faelan placed his daughter back into the man's arms. "I respect why you felt you needed to sue for custody and I don't hold it against you. I'm grateful you care about her well-being, but I am here now."

The man snorted, still not convinced.

Faelan tickled her tiny feet and smiled at her. "I know Kylie wants our daughter to have a close relationship with her grandparents, and I won't stand in the way of that as long as we understand each other. I am her parent."

Kylie's mother stepped forward to hold the baby. With tears in her eyes, she whimpered, "We only want what's best for her."

"We are agreed on that," Faelan assured her.

When the baby started crying again, Faelan looked to Celestia. "Would you teach me how to feed Kaylee?"

Celestia smiled warmly. "I would love to."

After they left, an uncomfortable silence filled the room. Clearing his throat, Kylie's father told Marquis Gray, "I'm still not convinced he should be the one to raise her."

"Todd doesn't have to prove himself to anyone but his child," Marquis Gray answered.

Kylie's mother placed her hand on her husband's arm. "Even though I hate leaving her, I am certain that's what Kylie would want."

He frowned. "We'll be watching him like a hawk."

Marquis Gray looked him directly in the eyes. "As long as you judge Todd Wallace with the same grace you were given as new parents."

Kylie's mother turned to him. "Mr. Gray, I shouldn't have slapped you. It was the heat of the moment."

He faced her, replying firmly, "Although I did nothing to deserve such treatment, I forgive you."

She looked at him meekly and nodded.

Gesturing toward the front door, he told them both, "Give the two of them time to connect."

Kylie's mother sighed heavily and kept glancing back. Brie could tell she was reluctant to leave even as Marquis Gray escorted them out.

Brie followed behind them and was surprised when she didn't see Mary or Lea waiting for her on the front porch.

After shutting the door, Marquis Gray turned to face Brie. "I didn't expect to see you here, Mrs. Davis."

Brie blushed. "Mary called and insisted I come. But I don't know where she and Lea disappeared off to."

"Ms. Taylor is here as well?" He looked surprised.

Shrugging, she told him, "Well, they *were* when I got here. They offered to watch my children while I spoke to Kylie's parents."

From the back of the house, Brie heard Mary call out, "Did those motherfuckers finally leave?"

Marquis Gray stared at Mary as she and Lea walked into the room.

"Apparently, you called in the cavalry when the police would have been a better choice."

Looking around the room frantically, Mary cried, "Did they snag the kid?"

Brie was just about to answer when Faelan stepped out of the nursery carrying his daughter.

Mary stopped dead in her tracks and stared at him as if she were seeing a ghost. "Where…where did you come from?"

"A few days ago Marquis warned me that things were starting to heat up with Kylie's parents. Durov insisted I fly back before it escalated into something."

He then glanced at Marquis. "Looks like I barely got here in time."

"I would never have let them take the child," Marquis Gray told him.

Faelan put his hand on his shoulder and said gratefully, "I know, Asher."

He turned to Brie. "Thanks for defending me back there."

She smiled and nodded, still too shocked by his sudden appearance to speak.

Being charmingly blunt, Lea blurted out, "So, what happened with your missing eye?"

Faelan chuckled. "Durov set me up with an ocularist. He was quite insistent, even using the whole 'I owe you my life excuse' even though I didn't want it. But, after trying on the prosthetic, I decided if I'm going to take on the role as her father, I want to lose the pirate look for the kid's sake."

Lea shook her head in amazement, drawing closer to him so she could examine both eyes. "It looks so real, I can't really tell the difference."

Faelan didn't seem at all uncomfortable by Lea's close scrutiny. "Durov hooked me up with the best ocularist in the world."

"How does it feel?" Brie asked. Faelan had once told her how uncomfortable they were.

"Not too bad, surprisingly. The guy is not only a world-renown artist, but his prosthetics are the best out there. Once I put it in, it feels no worse than wearing my eyepatch."

During the whole conversation, Mary hung back, staring at Faelan but not saying a word.

Celestia joined them, smiling proudly at Faelan. "I can't tell you how wonderful it is to have you back, Todd."

He smiled at her. "I'm grateful to you for taking care of her."

Celestia held out her hand to Mary. "Mary has been a godsend, helping us whenever she can."

"Really?" Faelan looked at Mary in surprise, shaking his head. "I thought you hated children."

She shrugged. "I still do."

"Oh, don't listen to her," Celestia laughed. "Mary's a

natural with Grace…I mean Kaylee."

"Kaylee?" Lea asked. "I thought you named her Grace."

Faelan explained, "I decided to give her a name that would honor her mother but still allow her to carve out her own path in life."

He turned to Marquis Gray and Celestia. "But, I wanted to keep Grace as her middle name in honor of the grace you've shown me and my little girl."

"No need to thank us," Marquis assured him, wrapping an arm around Celestia. "We knew it was our calling, and we were happy to stand in for you."

Celestia nodded, smiling at Faelan. "I knew you would come back. And, just look at you now. It's like you're a whole new man."

"I agree," Mary chimed in.

Faelan chuckled. "Sorry to disappoint you. Same flawed man, just rougher around the edges."

"That's untrue. You're stronger than before and have a deeper level of compassion for others," Marquis Gray stated.

"I don't know about all that, Asher." He sighed sadly. "All I really want is to be a good dad so I can look Kylie in the eye when I see her."

Marquis Gray's gaze softened. "That's an admirable goal."

Secrets Kept

"Well, I'm headed out," Mary suddenly announced, handing Hope to Brie.

"I am, too," Brie agreed, smiling at Faelan and the baby. "You need some uninterrupted daddy-daughter time."

"No need to see us all out," Lea told Celestia as she followed Brie to the front door.

Once they were outside, Lea said, "Was that crazy or what!"

"I can't tell you how much I was freaking out when Kylie's dad grabbed the baby," Brie told them.

"Oh, my God, what happened?" Lea asked, repositioning Anthony when he started squirming in her arms. We were trying to listen in at the back door but couldn't get close enough to hear what was being said."

"I seriously couldn't believe it when that woman slapped Marquis's face. Why don't I tell you guys all about it at my place since Anthony could use a nap?"

Mary frowned. "I gotta go."

Brie shot Lea a worried glance as Mary headed to her car.

"Maybe we can meet up tomorrow?" Lea asked Mary.

Mary waved her hand dismissively without looking back. "Whatever…"

"Hey, Mary!" Brie called out.

Mary turned and growled in irritation. "What?"

"Thanks for calling us."

Mary shrugged. "Later, losers."

Lea chuckled as they watched Mary get in her car and drive away. "You know, some people never change."

Brie nodded, even though she sensed something was definitely going on with Mary. From the moment she'd seen Faelan, her attitude had completely changed.

It worried Brie.

Brie was tickled to spend the afternoon at home with Lea. It had been a while since they'd spent any quality time together. After feeding Anthony and putting him down for his nap, Brie headed downstairs to find Lea on the floor building towers of blocks with Hope.

"You know, your two-year-old totally smokes me in the architecture department," Lea laughed.

Brie beamed at her daughter. "She amazes me every day."

"Did you know I got called pretty yesterday? It felt so good!" Lea giggled. "Actually, the full sentence was

'You're a pretty bad architect,' but I'm choosing to focus on the positive."

Brie shook her head. "You really *do* have a bad joke for every occasion."

"Great jokes," Lea corrected, placing a block on top of her tower just before it collapsed to the floor.

Hope laughed and held up a block to her, wanting her to do it again.

"At least I can make your kiddo laugh."

"So, tell me…" Brie prodded. "How are things with Hunter these days?"

The glow on Lea's face said everything before she even spoke. "I'm head over heels for the guy."

"And he feels the same?"

Lea's smile grew even wider when she squeaked, "Yeah!"

Brie grinned. "Is there a collar in your future?"

Lea's blush deepened to a redder color and crept down to her ample cleavage. "I think Hunter is planning something special."

Brie knelt beside Lea to give her a hug. "That's wonderful news. I'm so happy for you both!"

"Sometimes, I'm scared to believe it's real," she confessed. "After what happened with Samantha…and then Liam…" She looked at Brie sadly. "I kinda lost hope."

Brie gave her friend another tight squeeze. "You deserve only the best, and Master Nosh said Hunter was his top student. You seriously can't do any better than that."

"Don't tell anyone. I don't want to spoil what he's planning."

Brie made a zipper motion across her mouth. "My lips are sealed."

Lea laughed with glee. "I can't believe it's really happening. My happily ever after is coming true!"

"It couldn't happen to a better person," Brie told her with sincerity. "Hunter is a lucky man."

Lea sighed contentedly. "Do you know what vegetable this little submissive loves most?"

Brie shook her head.

"*Collared* greens!"

Brie groaned and then looked at Hope. "Your Aunt Lea is hopeless, sweet pea."

Lea rubbed the top of Hope's curly head. "Don't listen to your mommy. I'm full of the best jokes, and I plan to teach you every one."

"Don't you dare!" she laughed.

Brie was startled when she heard the front door open. "What's with all the laughter?" Sir asked as he strode into the room. As soon as he saw Lea, he chuckled. "Well, that explains it."

He glanced at Brie. "I'm sorry to break up this girl fest, but I'm headed to Anderson's and wondered if you wanted to tag along with me."

Brie's eyes lit up, touched by his thoughtfulness, then turned to Lea and grinned. "As much as I would love to, Sir, I just got Lea to myself."

"I have an idea," Lea told her, smiling at Hope. "What if I stay and hang with your kiddos? You can repay me with dinner when you get back."

Brie laughed. "I can't let you do that."

"What? You don't think I can handle it?" Lea challenged.

"Of course you can."

"Then go off with your Master and say hi to Shadow's family for me while you're there."

"You sure?"

Lea frowned. "You really don't think I can do it, do you?"

Brie put her hands up. "Have at it, my friend. Feel free to spoil my kids rotten but keep your jokes to yourself."

Lea looked at her in disbelief. "And, all this time, I thought you were a nice person."

Brie giggled, leaning down to give Hope a kiss. "Be good for Auntie Lea."

Hugging Lea again, Brie told her gratefully, "Thanks, girlfriend. I'll be sure to spoil *you* when I get back."

"You do that, Stinky Cheese."

Sir informed Lea, "We shouldn't be long. Anderson mentioned wanting to talk about something, but I can't see it taking long."

"Take all the time you need, Sir Davis."

As they were heading to the car, Sir asked Brie, "What was that all about? Since when does Lea want to watch our children?"

She smiled at him. "I think Lea wants to prove to herself that she can do it."

"Odd," he muttered as he opened the car door for her.

Brie suspected her friend was contemplating starting a family of her own and was testing the waters by watching two kids at once.

When Master Anderson opened the door, he seemed genuinely surprised to see her. "Ah, young Brie." He stepped aside, stating, "Well, it's good you're here. Getting a woman's perspective could prove useful."

Brie looked at him curiously as Sir escorted her inside.

"What's this about?" Sir asked. Brie knew he was as clueless as she was.

"Come sit while I run it by you."

They sat where he indicated. As soon as Sir put his whole weight on the cushion, a long fart sounded from underneath him.

Brie covered her mouth, giggling.

Sir gave him a deadpan look. "Seriously?"

Master Anderson slapped his thigh, laughing. "I couldn't resist, buddy."

When Sir went to stand up, Master Anderson pushed him back down forcibly. "You can't leave yet."

Although Sir seemed offended, Brie could tell by the telltale smirk on his lips that he secretly found Master Anderson's prank humorous. He would just never admit to it.

"All kidding aside, I've been considering taking a huge leap."

Sir cocked his head questioningly.

Master Anderson glanced at Brie and winked. "This is the biggest decision I've ever made and will impact my entire future."

Brie bit her lip, certain she knew what he was about to say.

Master Anderson sucked in his breath before blurting out, "I've been considering getting a dick reduction." When they started at him in shock, he added, "You know, like women do for breasts?"

Brie crinkled her brow, not expecting that.

After several seconds, he started laughing. "Like I would ever do that!"

Brie giggled, but she could see Sir's patience was running thin.

"You waited for us to return from Italy just to subject us to your meager attempts at humor?"

"No, buddy. But your reaction is priceless."

Standing up, Sir straightened his suit before turning to Brie and holding out his hand to her. "Shall we?"

"You can't go!" Master Anderson protested. "I'm just nervous is all. You can't blame a man for being nervous, can you?"

Sir frowned. "Cut to the chase, Anderson. I'm not in the mood for games."

"I totally hear you. So…" He rubbed his hands together nervously. "I've been giving it a lot of thought, and I feel the time has come to—"

The doorbell rang.

Master Anderson waved it off. "Whoever it is can come back later. Anyway…"

There was an insistent knock on the door.

Master Anderson growled. "Can't they just go away?"

When the doorbell rang again, Master Anderson

marched to the door and swung it open angrily. "What is so damn important?"

A small courier held up a large blue envelope. "I need a signature before I can leave."

Master Anderson cleared his throat and apologized before taking the pad, quickly signing his name, and handing it back.

After shutting the door, he stared down at the envelope as he walked back to them. Brie felt a spike of concern when she noticed his face had suddenly gone pale.

Sir's irritation was instantly washed away. "Who is that from?"

Master Anderson shook his head as he slowly sat down opposite them. "It's…a blast from the past."

Brie noticed his hand was shaking as he held the envelope.

"Who passed away?" Sir asked gently.

Master Anderson looked at him sorrowfully. "How did you know?"

"I understand the significance of that type of legal envelope."

Master Anderson stared at it again, seemingly lost in his own thoughts. He even appeared to have forgotten they were there.

When Sir quietly took Brie's hand to leave, Master Anderson looked up at them and pleaded, "Don't go."

While they sat back down, he started opening the envelope, then stopped himself and looked at them. "There's a secret I've kept for years. No one knows, not even my parents." Master Anderson sighed heavily. "I need you to promise this stays between us on pain of death."

"Isn't that a little extreme?" Sir joked.

"No," he stated in a serious voice.

Sir glanced at Brie. She nodded, prepared to keep Master Anderson's secret till death.

"It stays between us," Sir assured him.

Master Anderson took a deep breath before explaining, "All those years ago when you left college to fly to Russia to search for Durov, I met a man." Sadness seemed to wash over him when he added, "He was the greatest man I have ever met…"

"What happened?" Brie asked.

"He offered to mentor me." Master Anderson looked up and smiled at Brie sadly. "His name was Dominus Istvan Tóth. That man not only taught me to be a better Dom, but he also helped me save my family's ranch."

He glanced at Sir. "Dominus changed my future."

Sir shook his head. "Why is this the first I've ever heard of him?"

Master Anderson shrugged apologetically. "You were gone when I met him. Then I became consumed with trying to save my family's legacy. He became my lifeline."

"Your family almost lost the ranch?" Sir gaped in disbelief. "Why would you keep that from me?

"My father couldn't have handled the shame of people knowing Morning Wood was drowning in debt."

Sir suddenly seemed to make a connection and snapped his fingers. "*That's* why you went for the double major and became so focused on college."

Master Anderson nodded, chuckling sadly. "I nearly killed myself."

"I couldn't understand why you were working at the cafeteria while carrying such a heavy schedule."

Master Anderson gave him a half-smile. "Someone had to pay the ranch hand."

"Damn it, man. You should have told me."

"Why? What could you have done? You had enough on your plate as it was. Hell, the three of us were all just trying to keep our heads above water."

Sir frowned. "I hate knowing you suffered alone."

"But I didn't. Dominus met with me every week over a meal. I swear he and his four subs taught me more than I ever learned in college."

"Four subs?" Brie laughed in disbelief.

Master Anderson smiled. "Incredible women, each one of them."

He sighed heavily, sweeping his hair back. "God, I miss that man…"

Staring at the envelope, he told them, "For the life of me, I can't understand why I am getting this now." Grief darkened his eyes when he shared, "He passed away a year after I met him. No one knew he was dying, not even his subs."

"I can't imagine how hard it must have been to lose him unexpectedly," Brie said with sympathy.

He shook his head, wiping away a tear. "Fucking hurt more than I can say." He stared at the envelope, stating, "But Dominus already gave me an inheritance back then. Why am I getting this now?"

He glanced at the two of them. "Just so you know,

that's the secret you swore to keep."

"Got it," Sir replied for them both.

Master Anderson sat back in his chair. "Can you imagine getting half a million dollars at the age of twenty-two?"

Sir chuckled. "What the hell did you buy with it?"

"That was the genius of Dominus," he answered. "His inheritance came with a clause that I was to use it as a buffer and pay it back to myself if I ever needed to dip into it. Having that money allowed me to be fearless in business."

Sir nodded in understanding. "I can see the power of that."

"Dominus was brilliant. I had every intention of introducing you to him someday, but I had no idea he would be gone so fast…" He shook his head again, then stared at the envelope. "And now, Dominus has come back to haunt me."

Master Anderson sighed and glanced at them. "I'm glad you're here."

Ripping open the top of the envelope, he pulled out a stack of legal papers. Brie took Sir's hand as they watched him scan them.

Instead of tears, Master Anderson started laughing. "Holy hell…"

Raising his head and grinning at them both, he said, "You are now looking at a millionaire—two million, to be exact." His amusement grew as he flipped through the papers. "Only Dominus would think to do this."

Master Anderson suddenly stood up and started pacing while he explained, "It's taken my father this long to pay off the loan he owed. He made the final payment last month."

"That is quite an accomplishment," Sir stated.

"It really is. The ranch was on the brink of ruin, and he fought every day, year after year, to become debt-free."

Master Anderson looked up at the heavens and laughed. "How could either of us have known what you were really up to, you clever genius?"

Smiling at the two of them, he explained, "All this time, I assumed my father was paying off the bank loan, but he wasn't.

The loan had been secured by Dominus before he passed away. Every penny we thought was going to the bank was actually being deposited into another account."

He laughed again, shaking his head in amusement. "That account was transferred to me the day my father made his final payment."

"That is incredible news!" Brie cried.

"The absolute kicker is…" He chuckled as he pulled out a paper and showed it to them. "…at the time, I was strapped for cash and couldn't pay for the plane ride back to Colorado to make my pitch to the bank. When he offered to pay for my plane ticket, I told Dominus I was like my father who refused to take handouts. He agreed to honor my request, saying I could pay him back at a later date."

Pointing to the paperwork, Master Anderson laughed even louder. "Dominus deducted that exact amount from the total of my inheritance." Shaking his head, he grinned from ear to ear. "Dominus was a man of his word even after his death."

"Istvan Tóth sounds like an exceptional man. One we should all aspire to," Sir agreed.

"One hundred percent, buddy!"

Master Anderson's gaze drifted to his fireplace mantle. "Let me show you this."

He walked to the fireplace and picked up an intricately carved wooden box. "Martuska, one of his subs, made this. It's a Hungarian secret box."

Sir smiled as he took it from his friend, looking over the box with interest. "I've read about these but I've never seen one in person."

"They're supposed to have a secret compartment but, for the life of me, I've never been able to figure out how to open the damn thing," he admitted.

After studying it for a moment, Sir started fiddling with the box. Brie watched, transfixed, as he slid the bottom of the wooden box and moved a portion of the front panel to reveal a keyhole.

"Holy hell, how did you do that?"

Sir grinned. "I enjoy puzzles and was intrigued when I read about these particular boxes. Would you like me to find the key?"

"Yes!" Master Anderson told him, moving closer to watch.

After a few more adjustments, Sir revealed a small key and handed it to him.

Shaking his head in amazement, Master Anderson slid the metal key into the keyhole and unlocked the box.

When he opened the lid, Brie saw tears come to his eyes.

He pulled a photo from the secret compartment and stared at it for several moments before showing them. "This is Dominus, Edlyn, Jolan, Sarika, and Martuska—the woman who made the box."

Brie looked at the photo and saw a handsome man dressed in a fine suit. He had dark hair and a distinguished goatee. But, it was the smiles on the faces of his four submissives that caught her attention. Their expressions were so infectious, it made Brie smile just looking at them. "What a beautiful photo!"

Master Anderson nodded, his smile growing as he stared at the picture. "They made an incredible team, complementing each other with their many talents. Truly an amazing group of people."

He glanced at Sir. "Thank you for the gift of opening this box. I had no idea Martuska hid that photo inside." Tears suddenly came to his eyes. "Sorry, just feeling a little emotional seeing them again."

Sir stood up, setting the box on the coffee table. Taking Master Anderson's hand, he pulled him close and hugged him. "Trust me, Brad, I understand the power of old memories. There is no need to apologize."

Brie sat watching the two men. She realized there was a wealth of memories between them that she had yet to learn.

Master Anderson pulled away, picked up the paperwork, and stared at it as if he was contemplating something.

"Dominus made me promise not to tell anyone about the inheritance because he said I wouldn't be able to trust people's motivations or feelings toward me once they knew." Looking at the two of them, he added, "That's why you can't tell anyone about this."

"Understood," Sir replied.

"I won't say a word," Brie promised.

"Which brings me back to why I called you over in the first place." He paused and chuckled. "This kind of complicates things."

Sir looked at him curiously. "How so?"

Master Anderson grinned when he told them, "I've decided to ask for Shey's hand in marriage."

Brie jumped off the couch and ran to hug him. "You make such a cute couple! I wondered what was taking you so long."

He smiled warmly at her, then looked at Sir. "I was actually planning to ask if you would be willing to take covert pictures when I propose. I want to capture the moment without her suspecting a thing."

"Why me?" he asked in surprise.

"I remember the pictures you took that first semester in college. You're a natural."

Sir shook his head. "I'm sure you could find someone better, but I would be honored to act as your photographer."

"Good!"

He then looked at them both. "But that leads me to my next quandary. I hadn't planned to tell Shey about my half a million until after we were married. Now that it turns out I'm a millionaire, does that change things?"

Brie giggled. "What a crazy situation!"

"I don't think the amount plays into it," Sir told him seriously.

Master Anderson nodded. "Then I think I'll keep it as a surprise."

Staring hard at them both, he said, "But that means you take this secret to your graves."

"Of course," Sir agreed.

"I won't tell a soul," Brie vowed. "However, I'm grateful to know about Dominus and his four submissives."

Master Anderson smiled at her. "I'm glad to finally share them with someone." He stared at the photo again, lost in his memories.

"We should get going," Sir murmured to Brie.

Master Anderson nodded, only half-hearing him while he continued to stare at the old photo.

Letting themselves out, Sir put his arm around Brie as they strolled to the car. "I have to admit, that was the last thing I expected, but it explains so much…"

Brie felt like hugging herself, she was so happy. "Can you imagine waking up the morning after your wedding day to find out you are a millionaire?" She giggled when she thought about how surprised Shey would be when Master Anderson told her. But, just like Master Anderson, Shey would have to keep that a secret from everyone.

Brie was suddenly struck by a crazy thought.

How many other secrets are my friends keeping that I know nothing about?

Checkmate

B rie woke to find she was alone in bed.

Surprised, she slipped out from under the covers to search for Sir. But, before she made it out of the bedroom, she noticed that the door to their secret playroom was open.

Smiling to herself, Brie took a peek inside and saw the violet wand lying in the middle of their bondage table.

She shivered, knowing it was a hint of the type of scene Sir had planned for her. Brie hadn't felt the electric touch of the violet wand since Kinky Eve last year. The instrument had been off-limits to her the day she got pregnant.

Brie squeaked with excitement, loving that Sir was teasing her so early in the morning. Walking out of the bedroom, she found him in his office, typing on his computer. "Good morning, my sexy Sir."

He stopped and turned in his chair, smiling at her. "Today, I want you to free up your schedule to spend lunch with your Master."

"I can't wait," she answered, twisting where she stood. How was it that he could make her feel like a giddy sub just like that?

I'm such a lucky girl!

Brie spent the entire morning watching the clock, her panties getting wetter with each passing hour. When the appointed time finally came, Brie put the kids down for an early nap and tiptoed downstairs to find Sir waiting for her in the bedroom.

"Strip and kneel, téa."

She kept her gaze on him as she gracefully shed her clothes. Bowing her head, she slowly lowered herself to the floor, her entire body trembling with excitement. The simple ritual of kneeling before her Master was setting the scene before it even began.

When Sir approached and placed his hand on her head, she let out a breath of anticipation as she waited for his command.

"Stand and serve your Master."

When Brie stood, her whole focus centered on him and him alone.

Sir moved behind her, and she felt his fingers part her long hair down the middle before he began braiding one section of it. His hands were deceptively gentle as he did so, causing her to momentarily relax.

Sir ran his hand lightly over her entire back, causing goosebumps of pleasure to rise on her skin.

After braiding the other section, he commanded, "Follow me."

Brie's heart beat faster, his command reminding her

of the first night he'd led her to the bondage table at the Submissive Training Center.

After shutting the door, he swept Brie off her feet. Placing her on the table, he bound her face up, starting with her wrists. When he was finished, he asked, "Comfortable?"

The seductive tone of his voice made her quiver. "Yes, Master."

Sir ordered her to remain still.

Brie bit her lip when she heard the familiar electronic buzz of the violet wand. Sir turned the wand to its lowest setting and caressed her skin with it. The instrument tickled her with its electric touch.

There was no denying it was pleasant, and Brie let him know, voicing her pleasure by moaning softly.

He turned up the power a few moments later. Hearing the light crackling of electricity was thrilling, even if it was a bit intimidating. Brie held her breath as Sir grazed her skin with it.

The prickling sensation was more intense, but still pleasurable, making her moan even louder.

Sir glided it over the curve of both breasts, before grazing her stomach and thighs with the instrument. Sir then skillfully teased her with the violet wand, making her crave its electrified touch.

That's when the challenge began.

Sir smiled as he increased the power. Suddenly, the violet wand began crackling with wicked intent. Brie held her breath, waiting for the first contact at the higher power.

It was intense! She gasped as he dragged it down her

cleavage, her nipples instantly contracting into tight buds as he moved lower. Although she no longer found it pleasant, it was oddly erotic.

Brie watched with fearful anticipation as Sir lifted the wand and pressed it against her hard nipple. The electrical shock caused her to moan in pain and pleasure, her breathing now coming in rapid gasps.

He then grazed her inner thighs. Brie's entire body tingled under the challenging caress of his instrument. At one point, he turned off the lights in the room so she could watch the purple bolts of electricity shooting from the instrument to her skin.

Brie was mesmerized by it because it reminded her of the dancing flames of fire play.

"I see you like the challenge of the wand," Sir murmured seductively.

"I do, Master."

"Let me introduce you to its darker side."

Brie trembled as he turned the wand up to full power.

"At this frequency, it will feel like a knife cutting into your skin."

Brie stared at the violet wand fearfully.

"I want you to experience it," Sir told her.

Not being a masochist at heart, his challenge frightened Brie. The idea of willingly allowing herself to feel the cut of a knife was not sexy, even if the instrument would not actually slice into her skin.

Listening to the wand buzz at such a fierce frequency only made her decision that much harder.

"I know you will appreciate the experience, téa," he

encouraged her.

"Appreciate" and "enjoy" were two completely different things. She continued to stare at the violet wand, unable to make up her mind.

"You must want it for yourself," he stated. "I will not force you."

Brie took her eyes off the violet wand to look at him. The submissive in her longed to please her Master, but he was asking her to choose to experience pain of her own free will, not because he was willing it.

She realized that having to make that choice was the real challenge of this scene.

Brie closed her eyes and stilled her fears. Sir never expected her to exceed her limits. As long as she was true to herself, he would be pleased.

She knew if she ended the scene now, she would be left wondering what she had missed. Knowing herself too well, she opened her eyes and stated with conviction, "Please, Master."

"You have only to call your safeword and I'll stop."

"I understand, Master."

Brie knew that was the beauty and power of a safeword. Having control over the scene gave her the confidence she needed to face her own fears.

To her surprise, he turned off the wand. "I want you to close your eyes."

Brie nodded. Closing her eyes, she attempted to relax her body, forcing herself to breathe slowly as she waited for the intensity of the violet wand.

When he turned it back on at full force, the frightening sound caused goosebumps to rise on her skin. As much as she thought she was ready, Brie was not prepared for the sharp pain and screamed when she felt it.

The cruel intensity of the wand took her breath away as she felt the electrical current pierce her skin. As much as she tried, Brie could not convince herself that he wasn't leaving a long bloody gash down her stomach.

She immediately opened her eyes and called red.

Sir turned off the toy. "Are we done, then?"

Brie shook her head slowly. "I…I just needed to see my stomach."

He chuckled, giving her permission to look. Brie lifted her head and stared at her stomach in disbelief. It remained unharmed and without so much as a scratch.

She laid her head back down, still not quite believing it.

"One more pass?" Sir asked.

Enjoying the mindfuck aspect of this scene, Brie nodded.

Once again, Sir turned it to full power. He slowly dragged it from her stomach down to the crest of her mound.

Brie held her breath the entire time, both turned on and frightened by the pain.

When he finally turned it off, Sir looked at her proudly. "Well done, téa. I think your bravery deserves to be rewarded."

Brie smiled up at him, tears still pricking her eyes.

Sir quickly shed his clothes, joining her on the bondage table. With her body flying from the sub-high caused by the wand, she was extra sensitive to contact. Every touch, no matter how slight, sent a shiver through her.

When he settled between her legs and thrust his cock into her pussy, Brie shuddered in pleasure. "It won't take long," he murmured as he kissed her.

She nodded, already feeling the tingles of an impending orgasm sneaking up on her.

"Shall we go for four or five this session?" he asked as he changed angles to better stimulate her G-spot with the head of his cock.

She looked up at him in wonder, knowing her bliss was close at hand. Being a greedy little sub, she answered, "Five."

"As you wish," he growled as he ramped up his thrusts…

Sir sent Brie out shopping for the rest of the day while he stayed home to watch the children. Although she was grateful for his thoughtful gift, window shopping was never that much fun when she was all by herself.

Brie had just spied a Disney t-shirt of *Beauty and the Beast* and thought of Mary when she got a text from the woman herself.

Her ears must have been burning, Brie thought, laughing as she opened Mary's text.

We need to talk

Brie sighed. After Mary's strange reaction to Faelan a few days ago, she was worried Mary was hoping to rekindle things with him.

I've got some free time. What do you want to talk

about?

Meet me at the Egyptian Theater in Hollywood and I'll tell you

Brie smiled, relieved that Mary wanted to meet at a theater instead of the coffee shop. She took that as a good sign and felt a surge of excitement. The Egyptian was known for screening indie films, which was something Brie loved.

She quickly texted back, **What time?**

I'm here now

Brie looked up the address on her phone and gave Mary her ETA. **Looks like I can be there in forty minutes.**

Perfect, I've got a surprise for you

Watching an indie film with Mary sounded way more fun than wandering the outdoor mall alone.

Brie texted Sir to let him know her change of plans before heading out.

She was ecstatic when she arrived several minutes early and found a parking spot right away. Neither of those things had ever happened for her in Los Angeles.

Heading into the theater, Brie looked around for Mary. When she didn't see her in the lobby, she went to the ticket window. "Have you seen Mary Wilson? She's a tall blonde—"

"Oh, I know her," the guy assured Brie, raising his eyebrows suggestively. "Only the hottest thing in Hollywood."

Brie rolled her eyes. "Have you seen her here? We're supposed to meet up."

"Head into the theater," he told her, pointing to the door.

Brie pulled out her wallet, but when she tried to pay for her ticket, he refused to take her credit card. "It's already taken care of."

"Aww, that's sweet of Mary."

The door creaked as Brie opened it. She walked into the darkened theater and smiled, instantly recognizing the film on the big screen.

Walking down the middle aisle, Brie looked up to watch the flogging scene between Marquis and Lea from her first documentary.

To her surprise, she seemed to be the only one in the theater and called out, "Mary?" When she got no response, she called out again. "Mary, where are you?"

The film suddenly stopped mid-scene and the theater went pitch black.

Ice coursed through Brie's veins as she stood there alone in the dark.

"Mary?"

She heard movement just to the left of her.

Before she could turn, someone slid up behind her and covered her mouth with their hand.

Brie let out a muffled scream of sheer terror when she heard the familiar voice whisper in her ear.

"Hello, Brianna Bennet."

I hope you enjoyed *A Heart Unchained!*

COMING UP NEXT
Whispered Promises:
Brie's Submission Book 24
(Coming 2022)

The next book in the Brie Series will steal your breath away.

Get ready for the fireworks to begin…

COMING NEXT

Whispered Promises

Brie's Submission Book 24

Available for Preorder

Reviews mean the world to me!

I truly appreciate you taking the time to review
A Heart Unchained.

If you could leave a review on both Goodreads and the
site where you purchased this book from, I would be so
grateful. Sincerely, ~Red

ABOUT THE AUTHOR

Over Two Million readers have enjoyed Red's stories

Red Phoenix – USA Today Bestselling Author
Winner of 8 Readers' Choice Awards

Hey Everyone!

I'm Red Phoenix, an author who also happens to be a submissive in real life. I wrote the Brie's Submission series because I wanted people everywhere to know just how much fun BDSM can be.

There is a huge cast of characters who are part of Brie's journey. The further you read into the story the more you learn about each one. I hope you grow to love Brie and the gang as much as I do.

They've become like family.

When I'm not writing, you can find me online with readers.

I heart my fans! ~Red

To find out more visit my Website

redphoenixauthor.com

Follow Me on BookBub

bookbub.com/authors/red-phoenix

Newsletter: Sign up

redphoenixauthor.com/newsletter-signup

Facebook: AuthorRedPhoenix

Twitter: @redphoenix69

Instagram: RedPhoenixAuthor

I invite you to join my reader Group!

facebook.com/groups/539875076052037

SIGN UP FOR MY NEWSLETTER
HERE FOR THE LATEST RED
PHOENIX UPDATES

FOLLOW ME ON INSTAGRAM
INSTAGRAM.COM/REDPHOENIXAUTHOR

SALES, GIVEAWAYS, NEW
RELEASES, PREORDER LINKS,
AND MORE!
SIGN UP HERE
REDPHOENIXAUTHOR.COM/NEWSLETTER-
SIGNUP

Red Phoenix is the author of:

Brie's Submission Series:
Teach Me #1
Love Me #2
Catch Me #3
Try Me #4
Protect Me #5
Hold Me #6
Surprise Me #7
Trust Me #8
Claim Me #9
Enchant Me #10
A Cowboy's Heart #11
Breathe with Me #12
Her Russian Knight #13
Under His Protection #14
Her Russian Returns #15
In Sir's Arms #16
Bound by Love #17
Tied to Hope #18
Hope's First Christmas #19
Secrets of the Heart #20
Her Sweet Surrender #21
The Ties That Bind #22
A Heart Unchained #23
Whispered Promises #24

***You can also purchase the** AUDIO BOOK **Versions**

Also part of the Submissive Training Center world:

Rise of the Dominates Trilogy
Sir's Rise
Master's Fate
The Russian Reborn

Captain's Duet
Safe Haven #1
Destined to Dominate #2

Unleashed Series
The Russian Unleashed #1
The Cowboy's Secret #2

Other Books by Red Phoenix

Blissfully Undone
* Available in eBook and paperback

(Snowy Fun—Two people find themselves snowbound in a cabin where hidden love can flourish, taking one couple on a sensual journey into ménage à trois)

His Scottish Pet: Dom of the Ages
* Available in eBook and paperback

Audio Book: *His Scottish Pet: Dom of the Ages*

(Scottish Dom—A sexy Dom escapes to Scotland in the late 1400s. He encounters a waif who has the potential to free him from his tragic curse)

The Only One
* Available in eBook and paperback

(Sexual Adventures—Fate has other plans but he's not letting her go…she is the only one!)

Passion is for Lovers
* Available in eBook and paperback

(Super sexy novelettes—*In 9 Days, 9 Days and Counting, And Then He Saved Me,* and *Play With Me at Noon*)

Varick: The Reckoning
* Available in eBook and paperback

(Savory Vampire—A dark, sexy vampire story. The hero navigates the dangerous world he has been thrust into with lusty passion and a pure heart)

eBooks

Keeper of the Wolf Clan (Keeper of Wolves, #1)

(Sexual Secrets—A virginal werewolf must act as the clan's mysterious Keeper)

The Keeper Finds Her Mate (Keeper of Wolves, #2)

(Second Chances—A young she-wolf must choose between old ties or new beginnings)

The Keeper Unites the Alphas (Keeper of Wolves, #3)

(Serious Consequences—The young she-wolf is captured
by the rival clan)

Boxed Set: Keeper of Wolves Series (Books 1-3)

(Surprising Secrets—A secret so shocking it will rock
Layla's world. The young she-wolf is put in a position of
being able to save her werewolf clan or becoming the
reason for its destruction)

Socrates Inspires Cherry to Blossom

(Satisfying Surrender—A mature and curvaceous woman
becomes fascinated by an online Dom who has much to
teach her)

By the Light of the Scottish Moon

(Saving Love—Two lost souls, the Moon, a werewolf,
and a death wish…)

Play With Me at Noon

(Seeking Fulfillment—A desperate wife lives out her
fantasies by taking five different men in five days)

Connect with Red on Substance B

Substance B is a platform for independent authors to directly connect with their readers. Please visit Red's Substance B page where you can:

- Sign up for Red's newsletter
- Send a message to Red
- See all platforms where Red's books are sold

Visit Substance B today to learn more about your favorite independent authors.